THE
⊚™ MILLS & BOON®
Centenary Collection

**Celebrating 100 years of romance with
the very best of Mills & Boon**

*First published in Great Britain 2008
by Harlequin Mills & Boon Limited,
Eton House, 18-24 Paradise Road, Richmond, Surrey TW9 1SR*

© Sandra Myles 2001

ISBN: 978 0 263 86644 5

76-0908

*Harlequin Mills & Boon policy is to use papers that are
natural, renewable and recyclable products and made from
wood grown in sustainable forests. The logging and
manufacturing processes conform to the legal environmental
regulations of the country of origin.*

*Printed and bound in Spain
by Litografia Rosés S.A., Barcelona*

Malone's Vow

by
Sandra Marton

⊚™ MILLS & BOON®
Pure reading pleasure

Award-winning author **Sandra Marton** wrote her first novel while still at school. Her doting parents told her she'd be a writer someday and Sandra believed them. At high school and college, she wrote dark poetry nobody but her boyfriend understood. As a wife and mother, she devoted the little free time she had to writing murky short stories. Not even her boyfriend-turned-husband understood those. At last, Sandra decided she wanted to write about real people. That didn't actually happen because the heroes she created – and still creates – are larger than life, but both she and her readers around the world love them exactly that way. When she isn't at her computer, Sandra loves to bird-watch, walk in the woods and the desert, and travel. She can be as happy people-watching from a pavement café in Paris as she can be animal-watching in the forest behind her home in northeastern Connecticut. Her love for both worlds, the urban and the natural, is often reflected in her books.

You can visit Sandra Marton at her website at www.sandramarton.com

CHAPTER ONE

SHE WAS A BEAUTIFUL WOMAN, but not the kind a man should even consider marrying.

Not a man like Bill Thornton.

Liam Malone knew it the minute he saw her.

Bill wasn't her type. He was too good, too gentle, too trusting. He didn't stand a chance at being able to handle a woman like Jessica Warren. She was all quicksilver heat, while Bill was a glowing ember.

Hell, Liam thought as he stared out the window of Bill's study, past the rolling green lawn to Lake Washington glittering in the distance. He wasn't much given to thinking in metaphors, but that was what he'd thought of last night, at the rehearsal dinner. One look at his oldest friend's fiancée and he'd known Bill was making a big mistake.

Bill, of course, was clueless. He'd never been able to read women worth a damn. Liam always could. Jet-lagged as he'd been after the flight from Singapore to Seattle, one glance at his old friend's bride-to-be had told him everything he really didn't want to know.

"Wait until you meet Jessica," Bill had written in the letter that had followed Liam halfway around the world. "This is like a fairy tale, Liam, with me as the frog the beautiful princess turns into a prince. I still can't believe Jessica is going to be my wife."

Liam could. He'd spent enough years on the fringes of what most people called polite society to know that men and women married for lots of reasons, and hardly any had much connection to anything as banal as love.

More than one woman had called him a cynic, but Liam didn't agree. He was simply a realist. He understood that "love" was a catchall word people used instead of less poetic terms, especially in the rarefied strata of the very rich. Successful men married beautiful women as a balm to their egos. Beautiful women married successful men for the security of their wealth. He'd never sat in judgment on such arrangements. The trade-off was fair enough. It could work, assuming both parties to the deal were still willing to settle for those things a year or two into the marriage.

The men usually were. Arm candy was arm candy, after all. But the women often became restless. They wanted both jewels on their fingers and pleasure in their beds, and they went looking for it. One glance at Jessica Warren and Liam had known that Bill wouldn't satisfy her for very long. She'd need more than his kindness and money to keep her happy.

It would take more than that to keep her at all.

But the poor bastard didn't know it. He was marrying for love, and in his case, "love" really did mean a bucketful of syrupy clichés. One man, one woman. Forever after. Until death do us part. Bill was ready to swallow all of it, hook, line and sinker.

And that was the problem.

Give it a couple of years and Bill would still be crazy about his wife but she'd be bored to tears and looking for greener pastures. For all Liam knew, she was bored already. The flash in her eyes last night, when she'd caught him watching her, had said it all. She'd managed a nice girlish blush and a quick downward sweep of her lashes, but that hadn't changed anything. She'd been interested. His best friend's bride-to-be, interested in another man, the night before her wedding.

Interested in him.

Liam's mouth thinned.

It wasn't the first time a woman with a rich man in her life had given him that kind of look. Not all that long ago, he'd been the guy with the looks that turned women on and the empty pockets that turned them off. He'd lived by a combination of luck and his wits, but even so, he'd refused those invitations. He wasn't into playing games with women who belonged to other men. At best, he'd found that kind of come-on amusing.

Not this time. A single glance from Bill's fiancée, and he'd felt himself respond.

"Damn," Liam muttered. He swung away from the window, tucked his hands into his pockets and paced the length of Bill's study.

Of course, he'd responded. What man wouldn't? The message in those eyes had been clear, a promise of satin sheets and silken skin, of heated whispers and sizzling caresses. In one swift instant, his brain had stripped away the expensive suit, undone the classically styled hair…

Well, why not? He wasn't a saint. He was a healthy, heterosexual, thirty-four-year-old male. Yes, she was Bill's fiancée but a man's hormones had a way of ignoring the niceties. He knew that just as surely as he knew that a woman who was signing on for a happy ending with one man shouldn't look at another the way Jessica Warren had looked at him.

The trouble was, he had no idea what to do about it. He couldn't collar Bill and say, "You can't go through with the wedding this morning. The marriage won't work."

Bill would laugh in his face. As far as he was concerned, Jessica was the only woman in the world. As soon as she'd gone to the powder room, he'd leaned in close and confided that he'd never been this happy in his life. Jessica was all the things he'd ever wanted. She was beautiful and good-natured; she was bright and charming. And when Liam had cautiously hinted that she was getting a good deal, too, that marrying a guy with an old family name and money wasn't exactly a bad thing for a woman, Bill had happily agreed.

"Everything Jessica has, Liam—her education, her career—she got on her own." His smile had turned soft and loving. "It's going to be a joy to spoil her—if she lets me."

She'd let him, Liam knew. She was, already. The rock on her finger, the expensive watch on her wrist…oh, yes,

Jessica Warren would let her husband spoil her. The sad part, or maybe the good part, depending on your point of view, was that Bill's gifts would make both of them happy, he to give them and she to receive them. The question was, would the jewels, the furs, the cars, be enough to keep the lady faithful?

Liam doubted it. He knew how this particular fairy tale would end, and he was helpless to do anything about it without telling Bill the way Jessica had looked at him…and the way he'd looked at her.

A muscle ticked in Liam's jaw. He picked up a decanter of brandy and poured some into a crystal snifter.

There had to be some way to protect his oldest friend. They'd met at Princeton, where they'd made a strange pair. Bill had probably been enrolled the day he was born. Old-line money and a family that had come over on the *Mayflower* tended to do that for a man. Liam, on the other hand, was at Princeton courtesy of a glib tongue and money from the U.S. Army. His great-great-who-knew-how-many-times-great-grandfather had come to America either to escape the Irish potato famine or the long arm of the law, depending on who was telling the tale. Money and status weren't exactly part of the Malone family history.

Liam smiled.

Still, he and Bill had clicked. They'd fallen easily into an older brother, younger brother relationship, especially after Bill lost his parents in a plane crash in his sophomore year. Bill had financial consultants but it was Liam, the man of the world, who'd counseled him about Life. Bill, for his part, had saved Liam's tail more than once. Liam had been plagued with something an endless succession of advisors had called "an attitude problem." Put simply, it meant he'd have been kicked out of college half a dozen times, if it hadn't been for Bill and his connections.

It was time to return the favor.

"It's good to see I can still read your mind at a hundred paces, Liam, my man."

Liam swung toward the door. Bill, resplendent in his morning coat and striped trousers, grinned at him.

"Can you?" Liam said, and managed a smile.

"Sure." Bill walked to where Liam stood, reached past him for the decanter and poured himself some brandy. "'What's Malone doing now?' I asked myself a minute ago." Smiling, Bill lifted his glass to Liam's. "'He's stalking around my study,' myself replied, 'fortifying himself with brandy while he works up to telling me I'm on the verge of making the biggest mistake of my life.'" Bill laughed at the look on Liam's face. "I'm right, aren't I?"

"Absolutely, as long as you've asked."

"I knew it. What else would a confirmed bachelor like you think on my wedding day?" Bill downed half his drink and grimaced. "I needed that. My stomach's been going up and down like an elevator all morning."

"Bill." Liam put down his snifter. "Look, I know you think you're in love with this girl…"

"Woman," Bill said, and grinned. "Jessica has very definite opinions on the male-female thing."

"Yes," Liam said coolly, "I'm sure she does."

"Wouldn't go out with me at all, even though we'd

been working together almost a year. Said it wasn't right for a woman to date her boss."

"But you managed to change her mind."

Bill didn't seem to hear the sarcasm in Liam's tone. "I did," he said, and gave a lopsided grin. "Bet you didn't think I could talk a woman who looks like that into dating a guy like me, huh?"

Liam's brows lifted. "This isn't your first brandy today, is it?"

"It's my first in this room," Bill said, and chuckled. "Hey, you'd be edgy, too, if you were about to take a wife."

"You don't know what you're doing," Liam said bluntly, and felt better for finally having spoken the truth.

Bill sighed, sank into his favorite leather armchair and sipped his brandy. "I wondered how long it would take you to get around to that."

"Well, dammit, what choice do I have? You're about to make the biggest mistake of your life—"

"See? I even got the wording right."

"Bill, I'm serious."

"So am I, Liam. I love Jessica and she loves me."

"You know nothing about her."

"I know everything about her. I told you, she's had to make her own way in life. Her father never managed to hold on to a dime. He died when Jess was eighteen and she lost her mother only a year later. She's never been married, she has a degree in business studies—"

"You know nothing about her," Liam insisted. "You've only been dating her for, what, four months?"

"Only because she wouldn't go out with me sooner."

"Are you sleeping with her?" Liam said brusquely.

Bill blushed. "Direct, as always, Malone. Why do you want to know?"

A good question, Liam thought, and came up with what wasn't quite an answer. "It's normal for a man and woman who love each other to share a bed."

"So?"

"So, if you haven't slept with her, maybe you should consider why."

"Liam, I know you've been with a lot of women but Jessica is—"

"Different. Yes, I figured you'd say that. Look, you have to know that there are women who use sex to snare a man."

"Well, Jessica hasn't. Not that it's any of your business, but she hasn't slept with me yet. I haven't asked her to. She's not that kind."

Liam snorted.

"She isn't, dammit!"

"There are all kinds of ways to use sex, Bill. Withholding it is only one of them."

"Oh, for…" Bill shot to his feet. "Listen to me, Liam. Jessica is about to become my wife. Keep that in mind when you talk about her."

"Dammit, Thornton, haven't you grown up at all? You're as naive as you were when you needed me to save your skinny tail from the weird babe with the purple hair. You were certain she was the love of your life, too, remember?"

"Oh, give me a break! I was eighteen, not thirty."

"And not much smarter, from what I can see."

Bill's mouth thinned. "Back off, okay? I love Jessica, and she loves me."

"What if it's your money she loves? Your name? The step up you'll give her by marrying her?"

"It isn't." Bill walked to Liam's side, smiled and clapped a hand lightly on his back. "She loves me for myself, hard as that may be for you to believe, considering that it's you, with your black Irish good looks, the ladies always drool over."

"Dammit, hear me out."

"No." Bill threw an arm around Liam's shoulders. "No, for once, Malone, *you* hear *me* out. This is love. The real thing, and don't judge it by your need to bed every good-looking female in sight, or by figuring a man with a bank account is always a hostage to his money."

Liam looked at his old friend. He thought of telling him he'd changed that attitude when he'd finally decided there were better ways to indulge a love of risk than on the fall of the cards, but then he'd have to explain more than that, and this wasn't the time to do it. Not on Bill's wedding day, and it looked as if this really was going to be his wedding day.

Hell. Maybe Bill was right. Maybe the marriage would work. The bottom line was that there was nothing more he could do, except hope he was around to help pick up the pieces if, and when, the time came.

"Liam?"

Liam looked up.

"You could, at least, try and look happy for me."

"Sure." Liam sighed. "I hope it works out. You know that."

"It will," Bill said solemnly. "Jess is the best thing that ever happened to me. Once you get to know her, you'll think so, too. Come on, get that sour look off your face and admit the truth. You're just jealous 'cause I've found the perfect woman."

Bill smiled. Liam tried to, and wondered if he'd succeeded. "I hope you're right."

"I know I am. Now, drink up, wish me luck and then get out there and do your duty. I fielded half a dozen phone calls after the rehearsal dinner last night, every last one from a lady aching to know more about my best man."

Liam grinned. "Only half a dozen?"

"All right, a dozen." Bill grinned, too, and touched his glass to Liam's. The men finished their brandy, put down the snifters and walked to the door together. "You know how come you're such a cynic, my man? It's because the ladies let you get away with murder."

"The Malone charm," Liam said lazily. "Love 'em and leave 'em, that's me."

"Yeah, well, sooner or later, you'll meet a woman like my Jessica and you'll change your tune."

"Sure," Liam answered, because an intelligent man always knew when it was time to admit defeat. "Maybe in the next century."

Bill laughed. "Go on out and charm the ladies."

Liam strolled through the house to the music room, where the ceremony would take place. Pink and white roses filled the air with their perfume, and strains of Vivaldi drifted from the library. A pair of bridesmaids, ethereally lovely in gowns of palest pink, flashed him welcoming smiles.

Welcoming smiles to what he knew was going to end in disaster.

Liam turned on his heel and made his way through the house and out a side door to a garden with narrow, hedge-lined paths winding through it. He'd done what he could to convince Bill he was making a mistake. He was his friend's best man, not his conscience.

From this moment on, everything was up to fate.

UPSTAIRS, in one of the guest suites of her fiancé's home—the home that would soon be hers—Jessica paced restlessly from one wall to the other.

She'd longed for a perfect wedding day, and she had one. Blue skies, bright sun, not a single cloud to obscure the silhouette of Mount Rainier on the horizon…rare things in Seattle, but then, this was a special day. She was marrying the man she loved.

"Fate has really smiled on you, Jess," her maid of honor had said just a little while ago.

It was true. Jessie had never put much stock in fate, but how else could she explain all the wonderful things that had happened in the past few months? She and William had gotten to know each other. Their mutual respect had become friendship, and friendship had become love.

Jessica looked at her reflection in the mirror and

smiled. How could the day be anything less than perfect? Not just the weather but everything. The music she and William had selected. The menu they'd planned. The vows they'd written together.

I, Jessica, do solemnly vow that I will love you, William, for the rest of my life, that I will always be at your side…

Her stomach did a slow, dangerous roll.

She was nervous, that was all. And that was normal. Everybody said so, from the seamstress who'd put a couple of quick darts into her ivory satin gown to the stylist who'd plaited tiny pink tea roses into her hair. Even Carrie, her maid of honor, had said the same thing when she saw Jessie's hands trembling.

"Butterflies," Carrie had assured her. "All brides have them."

Where *was* Carrie, anyway? How long could it take to look for a bridal bouquet? Jessica glanced at the platinum-and-diamond watch William had given to her last night at the rehearsal dinner. "Something new," he'd said softly. The "something old" was the emerald-and-diamond engagement ring on her finger, which had belonged to his mother and grandmother.

The watch had caught her completely by surprise.

"Oh, it's too much," she'd blurted when she opened the long blue box and saw the wink of diamonds. William had laughed, kissed her gently and said that nothing was too much where she was concerned.

"I love you, Jess," he'd said softly.

Jessica swallowed dryly. She loved him, too. Her fiancé was a kind, generous, wonderful man and she was the luckiest woman in the world, and yes, the day really was going to be perfect…if she could just stop trembling.

"Butterflies," Jessie whispered to her image in the mirror. "All brides have them."

Was that true? She didn't know much about brides, perhaps because she'd never thought she'd be one, not after watching her mother endure a marriage to a man who'd made a mockery of the word. Jessie's father had been a handsome rogue. He couldn't stay in one place for very long or, as it turned out, be faithful to one woman, but her mother had adored him anyway.

Jessie grew up knowing she'd never be that kind of fool. Why would a woman have to be blinded by passion to fall in love? Love could be something that happened slowly and gently. That was the best way, the way that would last.

She smiled.

That was the way she'd fallen in love with William.

She'd worked for him for almost a year before he'd asked her out and even then, she'd turned him down. She knew that dating your boss was never a good idea, but he'd been gently persistent and, at last, after a late night at the office, she'd agreed to dinner. Saying no under those circumstances would have been silly. Soon they'd begun spending all their time together. When he'd proposed, saying yes had been the most natural thing in the world.

Now she was less than an hour away from becoming Mrs. William Thornton the Third. It was hard to believe it was happening.

One man, one exchange of vows, for the rest of her life.

Maybe it wasn't fashionable to believe in forever-after anymore, but Jessie did. It worried her a little that she'd never yet wanted more than William's tender good-night kisses, but she was sure that would change. Given time, her skin would tingle when he touched her. Just looking at him would make her breathless. She'd feel the way she'd felt last night, when she'd first laid eyes on Liam Malone.

Jessie took a step back, felt the bed hit behind her knees and sank down on the edge of it.

"Oh, God," she whispered, and shut her eyes as if she could block out the memory. What was she doing, thinking about another man on her wedding day? She hadn't even been looking forward to meeting Liam. William had talked about him endlessly, until she'd been weary of hearing the name and the stories that went with it. How Liam traveled the world. How he made fortunes and lost them on the turn of a card. How he went through women. She'd been appalled by some of the stories, fascinated by others and aware, almost immediately, that her sweet, sensible William was wistfully envious of Liam's free and easy life.

She'd come up with a picture to go with the tall tales. Liam would be sexy as sin, gorgeous as the devil and twice as persuasive. In other words, he'd be the kind of man she most disliked.

As it turned out, she'd gotten it almost all right. The rehearsal dinner had been in full swing; William had been holding her hand and telling her how happy they were going to be. Suddenly he'd dropped her hand, leaped from his chair and said, "Liam, my man, you made it!" She'd looked up and there, in the doorway, she'd seen Liam Malone for the very first time, exactly as she expected: tall, broad shouldered, with a handsome face, a shock of silky black hair and emerald-green eyes.

What she hadn't expected was the jolt of electricity that slammed through her when those green eyes met hers. Her heart had gone into overdrive and a pervasive heat had slipped under her skin. She'd felt all the reactions she'd sworn she'd never feel for any man, and she'd felt them for her fiancé's best friend.

She'd wanted to bolt from her chair and run. Instead, she'd torn her eyes from Liam's, stared blindly down at the table, and hoped, prayed, that the floor would open up and swallow her.

"Jessica, sweetheart," she'd heard William say, and she'd forced herself to look up and smile. William had his arm slung around Liam's shoulders and he was smiling, too, but Liam hadn't smiled at all. He'd just watched her through narrowed eyes set in a face that might have been chiseled from granite.

Somehow she'd stood up, said all the right things, extended her hand and tried not to jump at the tiny spark that leaped from Liam's fingers to hers.

"Static electricity," she'd said with a forced laugh.

"Indeed," Liam had replied, and the slightest smile had curved his mouth, a smile that said he knew exactly what she was feeling. "It's a pleasure to meet you at last, Jessica."

And that had been the end of it.

Jessie let out a breath she hadn't realized she'd been holding.

What was the matter with her? That *had* been the end of it. The moment had come and gone. Liam pulled up a chair, William settled in beside her again, and she'd listened while the two friends talked about old times. Her gaze had met Liam's once again but she'd looked quickly away and, before she knew it, the evening ended. Come stay with us, William had said, and she'd found herself fearing the answer, but Liam had thanked him politely, said he already had found a place and went off to wherever it was.

"A hostel, for all I know," William had said cheerfully, "or a penthouse. It depends on whether his luck's been good or bad."

Good, Jessie thought now, remembering the expensive cut of Liam Malone's gray suit. Or maybe bad, considering the longer-than-it-should-have-been, black-as-midnight hair that curled over his collar. She thought, too, of what William had told her, that Liam liked to gamble. Poker was his specialty, William said, but Jessie knew that women would be Liam Malone's specialty, women who were willing to trade one night in his bed for a lifetime of hot memories.

She stood up quickly and smoothed down her skirt. Where was Carrie? Better still, where was William? She needed to see him, put her hand in his, feel the warmth of his smile.

"Got 'em!"

Jessie swung around. Her maid of honor stood in the

doorway, holding a bouquet of tiny pink roses, trailing baby orchids and lacy-white stephanotis in her hand.

"Would you believe the kid who delivered the flowers left your bouquet on a table in the—"

"Have you seen William?" Jessie hadn't meant to sound so shaky, but the look on Carrie's face told her she hadn't succeeded.

"What's the matter, Jess?"

"Nothing. I just want to see him, that's all."

"You can't see him. It's bad luck for the bride and the groom to see each other before the ceremony."

It was worse luck to think about another man before the ceremony, but Jessie knew better than to say that.

"That's just a silly superstition."

"Maybe, but do you really want to tempt fate?"

"No." Jessie gave a choked laugh. "That's the last thing I want to do."

"Jess." Carrie's voice softened. "Honey, I keep telling you, all brides are jittery."

"I know. And I'm not jittery. I just—I need some fresh air." Jessie gathered up her skirt so the hem wouldn't drag. "I'm going for a walk in the garden."

"What?" Carrie stared at her as if she'd lost her mind. "You can't! It's only half an hour until the ceremony."

"That's plenty of time."

"What if someone sees you?"

"Nobody will. I'll go down the back stairs."

"But—but you'll get grass stains on the hem of your gown."

"I won't. See?" Jessie hoisted the gown higher.

Carrie sighed. "Well, who am I to argue with the bride? You want to go for a walk? Fine. We'll go for a walk."

"No!" Jessie swallowed hard. "No," she said, more calmly, "really, I need a few minutes by myself."

"It's cold outside," Carrie said worriedly. "At least take a jacket."

"It's okay," Jessie said, "I know what I'm doing."

But she didn't. And the enormity of the lie scared the life out of her.

THE GARDEN WAS QUIET. All the hullabaloo was taking place inside the house. Liam was glad he'd decided to go for a walk where he could escape the necessity for social niceties.

He felt a lot better, too. For all he knew, Bill was right. Maybe he'd misread everything. The newlyweds would settle into a pleasantly dull marriage. A couple of years down the road he'd look at Jessica and know that he'd been wrong about her.

But if he was, then what was that invitation he'd seen in her eyes last night? What would she have done if he'd taken her up on it, if he'd walked straight across the room, pulled her out of her chair and kissed her?

Slugged him, probably, because whatever else the lady was, she wasn't a fool. Bill would have slugged him, too, but at least he'd have learned if that soft, pink mouth tasted as sweet as it—

There was a whisper of sound just behind him. Liam drew a breath. Even before he turned around, he knew she'd be there.

"Miss Warren," he said with deliberate courtesy.

Her chin lifted, her cheeks pinkened. Could she possibly know what he'd been thinking?

"Mr. Malone," she said, just as courteously. "I didn't expect to find you here."

His smile didn't reach his eyes. "Is it customary for brides to wander around, alone, moments before they wed?"

"I might ask you the same question about groomsmen. What are you doing in the garden?"

Liam looked at the woman who was about to marry his best friend, into the smoky blue eyes that had haunted him through a long and sleepless night.

"Looking for you," he said, and before she could respond, he reached for her.

CHAPTER TWO

PEOPLE ALWAYS TALKED about time standing still or going too fast, but in Jessie's experience, time was more like a treadmill. It moved at a steady, predictable pace.

Now she knew she'd been wrong. Liam reached for her and time hung suspended by a silken thread. She had all the opportunity she needed to anticipate what was about to happen. He was going to take her in his arms, gather her close and kiss her. And she'd let him do it. The dreams that had kept her awake half the night because, yes, she'd dreamed of him, yes, she'd imagined this happening… those dreams would come true.

She sighed, lifted her head, closed her eyes, waited to feel the hardness of Liam Malone's body, the race of his heart…

Waited to betray William.

She took a quick step back, her hands upraised. "No," she said, but it didn't stop him. Liam caught her hands, drew them down. "Liam," she said sharply, "think of William!"

He lifted his head and stared at her through eyes that were dark and hot. Slowly, like clouds receding after a storm, the wildness in his eyes faded. A shudder racked his body, and his hands fell to his sides.

"My God!" He spoke in a choked whisper. "We must be crazy."

Jessie opened her mouth, then closed it. The truth was ugly, but she couldn't deny it. She'd been a part of what had almost happened.

"Nothing happened." Panic lent her words harsh urgency. "Nothing," she repeated, as if saying it again would make it so.

"No." Liam nodded. He turned his back to her and she saw the rise and fall of his shoulders, heard the sound of breath being dragged deep into his lungs. "Nothing happened. And anyway, it didn't mean a…" He swung toward her, anger etched into his face. "The hell it didn't! I'm Bill's best man. You're his bride. And we almost went at each other like a pair of—of sex-starved teenagers. And you say, nothing happened?"

"Mr. Malone…"

"Oh, that's great. That's terrific. Another minute, we'd have been down on the grass and you're calling me 'Mr. Malone'?"

Jessie stiffened. "There's no need to be crude."

"Crude is you not remembering that you're marrying my best friend this morning."

A breeze rustled through dried autumn leaves still trapped in the hedge. Jessie shivered and wrapped her arms around herself.

"I remembered it, and so did you. That's why nothing happened."

"I came within a breath of betraying my friend. You came within inches of violating the promises you've made him. Seems to me that something happened."

The wind lifted a strand of Jessie's hair. Her hand trembled as she smoothed it back. He was right. They'd almost kissed. Pretending they hadn't wouldn't change the fact, but there had to be an explanation. She'd never hurt William. Never.

"All right." Her voice quavered. "But—but it's been a stressful week."

"Now, why didn't I think of that?" Liam said coldly. "You're stressed. I'm jet-lagged. And that makes it all…" He paused, then blew out a ragged breath. She was right. Nothing they could do would erase that one moment but, the truth was, they hadn't done anything. The best solution was to shove the memory into a dark corner and forget it was there.

"Okay. We made a mistake. Let's leave it at that."

"That's what I've been saying." Something in his eyes— contempt, perhaps, or a suggestion of it—stirred Jessie's anger. "And if you want to be specific, Mr. Malone, we didn't make a mistake. You did. I'm not the one who— who…"

"Do us both a favor, okay? Let's not waste time lying." His mouth twisted. "You and I both know what's going on here. You looked at me last night exactly the way you did a couple of minutes ago."

"I don't know what you're talking about." Jessie gathered up the skirt of her bridal gown. "And I have better things to do than stand here and talk nonsense."

"Yeah," Liam said coldly. "You have to step up to a judge, take Bill's hand and promise to love, honor and cherish till death—"

"I know the vows I'm going to take, Mr. Malone."

Liam's eyes narrowed until there was just the barest flash of green. "I thought you were all wrong for him. Now I know it."

"Is that what this—this little episode was all about? The Liam Malone quality control test?" Jessie said, trying to keep her tone as cold and even as his.

"Bill deserves better than you. A man deserves a woman who loves him without reservation."

"And that's just the way I love William," she said heatedly. "He knows that."

"Right." Liam smiled tightly and rocked back on his heels. "I'm sure he'd agree that the last few minutes prove it."

"You can't tell him! You'd break his heart!"

"I know that. No, I won't tell him. Neither will you. You're right. Nothing happened." He paused, and a seductive softness crept into his voice. "But it could have."

Jessie knew what he was thinking. How it would have been, if they'd kissed. The mingling of breath. The taste. The feel of his arms around her, the heat of their bodies pressed together.

"This is a pointless conversation," she said, and some small part of her mind gave a brisk nod of approval that she could sound so calm when she was shaking inside. "William is waiting. The wedding—"

Liam caught her wrist as she began to turn away. "Why didn't you slap me?"

"Mr. Malone. Liam. I thought we just agreed—"

"It's a simple question. You knew what I was about to do. How come you didn't haul off and slug me?"

"Is that how the women you come on to generally react?" She smiled sweetly before her lips hardened into a thin, accusing line. "I don't understand how William can think of you as his best friend. You're not like him at all."

"No," Liam said softly, "I'm not."

He took a step toward her; she retreated, but the bench was behind her and she was trapped. Her heart pounded. She'd been right about Liam Malone. He was sexy as sin and gorgeous as the devil. Why hadn't she realized he'd be as dangerous as the devil, too?

"Keep away from me!"

He smiled, a quick glint of white teeth against his tanned face. "Maybe that's what appeals to you, Jessie." Lazily he ran a finger over her cheek. "Maybe you know there's no way you could wrap me around your little finger, or buy me off with a smile and a promise."

"You're right. I should have slapped you. You're a horrible man."

"I must be," he whispered, his fingers curling around the back of her neck, "because I'm going to finish what I started a few minutes ago. What you want, despite all your self-righteous protests."

He watched her face as he drew her to him and told himself he was only doing this because she was twisting things, making it sound as if he were the only one who'd wanted the kiss. One whisper of dissent, just one, and he'd back off. But when she looked up at him, he saw that her eyes had gone from blue to the color of the sky just before sunrise in the mountains, and not all her protests or his excuses could keep those eyes from telling him everything he needed to know.

"Jessie," he said softly, and she sighed, tilted her head back and met his descending mouth with hers.

It was a gentle kiss, only the brush of his lips over hers. It was the kiss a man gives a woman when he knows he can never claim the taste of her again. And because the kiss was gentle, because Jessie knew that there would only be this once between them, because she could no more have stopped the rotation of the earth than rid herself of the need for it, she let it happen. She let him draw her closer, and when he did, she laid her palms flat against his chest, rose on her toes and parted her lips to his, let him slip his tongue into her mouth.

A wave of white-hot flame consumed her. She moaned, curled her fingers into the lapels of Liam's morning coat and let everything she'd spent the night dreaming about happen. His kiss was all the poets said a kiss could be. It was more. It was turning her inside out, dissolving her flesh, melting her bones. It was...

She lifted her arms, wound them around Liam's neck and stopped thinking.

The wind scurried through the garden again. Jessie trembled, but not from the cold. Liam drew her, hard, against him. His hands swept down her back, cupped her bottom, lifted her against him, into him. Sounds drifted on the air. Music from the chamber orchestra. The distant buzz of conversation.

And, from somewhere nearby, Carrie's voice.

"Jessica? Jess, where are you?"

Jessie tore her mouth from Liam's. Panic raced through her blood. "Liam!"

His arms tightened around her as she tried to pull away. "Come back here," he said thickly.

"Liam, for the love of God, someone's coming!"

He blinked, shook his head, whispered a word that might have been a blessing or an oath and stepped back, as if putting distance between them could change what had happened.

"I didn't…" He stopped, cleared his throat. "Jessie, I never meant—I never meant this to happen."

"Then—then it didn't," she said frantically. "Do you hear me? This never happened." Her lips felt dry. She touched them with the tip of her tongue, tasted Liam and felt as if she wanted to die. "William must never find out. Do you understand?"

"Dammit," Liam said harshly, "don't you think I know that? But we can't just forget. We—"

"Jess?"

Jessie spun around. Carrie stood a few feet away, staring at them. "Everyone is waiting," she said slowly. "The judge. The guests. William."

"Of course." Jessie gave in to the temptation to touch her hand to her hair. She could feel some strands that had come undone, but the wind could have done that. Only the wind. She'd simply been out here, having a pleasant chat with William's best man. Nobody had to know the truth, not ever. Nobody but Liam. And she. Oh God, she would know, she'd always know. "Certainly," she said, and smiled. "I'm ready."

Carrie cleared her throat. "I think—why don't you just let me fix your makeup, Jess? Your lipstick. And your hair. The, uh, the wind must have…" Her voice trailed away as she hurried forward and clasped Jessie's arm. "Come on up to the house, okay?" She smiled brightly. "A bride should look perfect on her wedding day. Isn't that right, Mr. Malone?"

Liam nodded. It was the best he could manage.

"Why don't you go tell William we'll just be another five minutes? He can wait that long for the woman who's going to be his for the rest of his life, don't you think?"

The message might have been subtle, but the way Jessie's maid of honor looked at him wasn't. Could what they'd done be so obvious? Liam cleared his throat and decided to see if he could get out something more than a croak.

"Yes," he said, "I'm sure he can."

"Good." Carrie wrapped an arm around Jessie's waist. "Now, come on, honey. This is your big day. You don't want to spoil it."

"No," Jessie said. "No, I don't."

Her eyes met Liam's, and the terrible secret they shared burned hot between them.

"Jess?" Carrie said, and Jessie smiled brightly and let her maid of honor hurry her toward the house.

Liam waited until they were out of sight. Then he let

out a breath that was almost a moan and ran his hands through his hair. How could he let her go? He'd only had one taste of Jessie, only held her in his arms for a moment.

"Stop it," he said in a harsh whisper.

He walked deeper into the garden, found a bench, sank down on it and put his face in his hands. How could he have done this? She was to be Bill's bride. Bill, who was the best friend he'd ever had. If only there were a way to wipe away what had happened.

But there wasn't. And the longer he thought about it, the more he knew that nothing could have stopped him from kissing her, or make him regret the kiss. Now he knew how soft Jessie felt. How sweet her lips were. How it was to take her sigh into his mouth as she opened to him.

How right he'd been in his assessment of her.

Damn Jessica Warren to hell, and himself along with her! How could he let her marry Bill? And yet, he had to. He couldn't tell Bill what had happened, not if saving him meant destroying him. Time slipped past as he tried to find a solution but, at last, he knew he had to admit there was none. He had to play his role in this farce. There was no other choice.

At last, Liam sat up straight. He had no idea how long he'd been sitting there but it was time to put a smile on his face and do what was expected of him.

Liam stood, smoothed down his shirt, took a couple of deep breaths.

"Liam?"

Bill was hurrying toward him, his face tense, and for one awful moment, Liam thought he'd found out what had happened. But Carrie was trotting alongside him, looking just as bad.

"What is it?"

"It's Jessica," William said. "She's—she's gone."

"What?" Liam eased an arm around Bill's shoulders, led him to a bench and sat him down. "What do you mean, she's gone?"

Carrie knelt on the grass and took Bill's hands in hers. She spoke to Liam, but her eyes never left Bill's pale face.

"She wrote a note," Carrie said, "and left it on the bed with her engagement ring and watch."

Liam shook his head. Maybe he wasn't crazy. Maybe it was the rest of the world that had gone insane. "Bill?" He squatted down beside the bench. "Talk to me. How can she be gone? Gone where?"

Bill took a piece of paper from his pocket and handed it to Liam. "You can see how upset she must have been," he said shakily. "Just look at how she scrawled the words."

Upset? Oh, yes, Liam thought as he took the note, yes, indeed, the lady would have been upset. Beside herself, was more like it, afraid—no, terrified—that he'd break his promise and tell Bill what had happened.

Dearest William: I'm sorry. So terribly sorry. You're a wonderful man. A fine man. That's why I can't marry you. You deserve more than I can ever give you. Forgive me, please.

He read the note again and again, until anguish blurred both his anger and the words Jessie had written. He had done this. He'd given in to a moment's desire and this was the result.

Slowly Liam rose to his feet.

"Carrie? You took Jessie back to the house. What happened after that?"

"I started to fix her hair, but she said she wanted to do it herself. She asked me to go downstairs and make sure everything was ready. When I got back, she was gone." Carrie gave Liam a look filled with loathing and accusation. "She was fine before she went out to the garden. Just bridal jitters, that was all. She was fine!"

Liam nodded. There was a bitter taste in his mouth. He'd come back to Seattle to join in a happy celebration. Instead, he'd kissed a woman who wasn't his to kiss, and now his best friend was behaving as if his life had ended. Like it or not, he knew what he had to do.

"Bill?" He squatted down again, put a hand on Bill's knee. "Bill, you have to go after her."

"Go where?" Bill looked up, his face tearstained. "She gave up her apartment when I asked her to move into the guest suite here."

"Well, what about family? Friends?"

"Jessica has no family. And her friends are all here, at the…in the house."

"Call the police," Carrie said. "Hire a private detective."

"No. No, I can't do that. Jess isn't a fugitive. She's my fiancée and if she's run away, it has to be my fault. I must have done something to make her—"

"You didn't," Liam said, so sharply that Bill stared at

him. "I mean, there's no reason to think that. You'd know if you'd done something to drive her away."

"The only thing I know is that I have to get her back." Bill clamped his lips together, bowed his head. Seconds passed before he looked up again. "Liam? You have to find her for me."

Liam shot to his feet. "No. Not me."

Bill stood up slowly, looking as if he'd aged five years in the past five minutes. "She'd run if she saw me. She has no reason to run from you."

"Bill," Liam said, "Bill, please—"

"And you know something about running away. You used to talk about it, remember? About how you'd run away all those times when you were a kid?"

"Yeah, but that was—"

"Let's be honest, okay? I'm—what's that phrase of yours? I'm a desk jockey. If I were going to run away, I'd probably tuck a couple of credit cards in my pocket and ring for the chauffeur to bring the car around." Bill gripped Liam's arm. "I'm afraid for her. I can't imagine where she'll go. Carrie says she didn't even change her clothes or take anything with her. What will she do for money?"

"She took her car," Carrie offered excitedly. "A white Civic. It's not in the driveway anymore."

"Well, then, she'll drive until she runs out of gas."

"Who knows where she'll be by then?" Bill's hand dug into Liam's flesh. "I'm begging you, man. You're like a brother to me, you know that. You've got to do it."

There'd been times in Liam's life when he hadn't much liked himself. He'd thought that those times were all behind him. But as he looked into the pleading eyes of his oldest friend, he knew he'd never hated himself as much as he did at this moment.

"All right," he said slowly, "I'll find her for you."

Bill expelled a breath. "Thank you."

"Don't thank me until this is over."

"I know you, Liam." Bill put out his hand. "You'll find my Jessica, and you'll do the right thing."

Liam looked at his oldest friend's outstretched hand, clasped it and forced a smile to his lips. "I'll do the right thing," he said softly. "I promise you that."

CHAPTER THREE

LIAM SAT BEHIND THE WHEEL of his rented Corvette as Bill leaned through the open window.

"Call me as soon as you find her, okay?"

"Look, I can't guarantee—"

"Tell her I love her, that whatever's wrong, we can work things out." He gripped Liam's shoulder. "I don't know how to thank you, man."

"Don't," Liam said quickly. "Not until I've brought Jessie back."

"Jessica." Bill's voice broke. "Her name is—"

"Sure." Liam shifted into gear. "I'll be in touch."

Bill said something else but Liam didn't wait to hear it. He stepped on the gas and the Vette's tires squealed as he shot down the long driveway. Another couple of minutes listening to Bill talk about Jessie and how he couldn't think of a reason in the world she'd have done this, and he'd have blurted out the truth.

"I know the reason," he'd have said. "It's because I violated our friendship and my principles over a woman I don't even know."

"Hell," he said softly, and clamped his hands more tightly on the steering wheel. If there was one thing he'd learned, it was that there was no percentage in reliving the past. You made a mistake, you set it right and you moved on. That was exactly what he was going to do. Find Jessie, make her see reason, return her to Bill and move on.

He drove fast, slipping in and out of traffic, heading for his hotel so he could trade his morning coat and striped trousers for something that wouldn't make him stand out in a crowd. The only thing as noticeable as a woman driving around in a bridal gown would be a man pursuing her rigged out in a silly suit. Besides, who knew what story Jessie might tell if people asked for explanations? The last thing he needed was interference from some helpful soul who might take him for the groom she was fleeing.

Liam dressed quickly, trading his formal wear for faded jeans, an ancient Princeton Tigers sweatshirt, sneakers and a leather bomber jacket he'd had so long that it felt like an old friend. Then he got into the Vette, doubled back toward Lake Washington and got on the road Jessie would have taken. An excited guest had told him she'd headed toward the city, but where would she go? No apartment, no credit cards, no cash…well, not exactly. Carrie had remembered that Jessie kept a fifty-dollar bill and her driver's license in the glove compartment of her car.

"Mad money, she called it," Carrie had explained, while Bill clutched her hand like a lifeline. "I always told her that was just making it easy for a thief, but—"

"It's okay," Liam had replied. "She won't get far on fifty bucks."

Now he tried putting himself in Jessie's place. What would she use the money for? Like him, she'd want to get out of that bridal regalia. And she'd want a place to go to ground, but in a city like Seattle, how could anybody afford clothes and a hotel room on fifty bucks? That was the question, although the bigger one was what he could possibly do or say when he found her to make her see that kiss for what it really was.

Liam glanced in his mirror, gave the Vette a little more gas and switched lanes.

It was simple, really. What had happened between them was lust. That good old male-female, down-and-dirty, I-want-to-get-you-between-the-sheets thing called lust. They'd been sexually attracted to each other, she'd been all nerves, and he'd taken advantage. End of story.

He wasn't a gentleman like Bill. And he couldn't let a moment's stupidity and weakness on his part ruin what Bill wanted. A wife, a couple of kids, a dog and a cat.

Some people were made for fairy tales.

Liam looked at the speedometer and eased his foot off the gas. He was driving too fast, and he could just imagine trying to explain this to a cop.

"Well, you see, Officer, I came on to my best friend's bride maybe ten minutes before the ceremony, and she ran away."

Oh, yeah. That would go over big.

Dammit, where had she gone? Forget the change of clothes. She was upset, probably close to hysterics by now. Her first priority would be a hotel room, but without money…

A horn blared as Liam shot across two lanes of traffic and made for the exit ramp. He looked in the mirror, saw the guy he'd cut off tell him what he thought with a universal gesture, and fought back the urge to respond. The guy was right. There was no need to be angry at him. Jessie, dammit, she was the one who'd made him lose control, made a mountain out of a molehill, ruined what should have been the best day of Bill's life, and for what?

"For a kiss," Liam said, with a snort of disbelief. Just a kiss. Just a moment torn out of time, when he'd held her in his arms and never wanted to let her go....

There she was!

He stood on the brakes, made a hard turn into a lot dominated by a huge Kmart, and brought the car to a jolting stop. A slender figure in ivory satin, little pink roses braided into her honey-gold hair, was marching— there was no other word for it—straight toward the store entrance, her satin train sweeping behind her.

Liam eased the car forward a safe distance, pulled into a space, shut off the engine and watched. Someplace between her car and the door, she'd picked up a gaggle of followers. Kids, a few housewives, a guy in coveralls, all of them shuffling after her, grinning at each other, peering around as if they suspected they might be on *Candid Camera*. Well, he couldn't blame them. A bride in full regalia, going into a store that sold everything from aspirin to zippers, was definitely not an everyday sight, even in a city as sophisticated as Seattle.

Jessie had to know she was drawing a crowd, but her

chin was up and her spine was as straight as it had been when she'd faced him down in the garden.

He got out of the car, pocketed his keys and started after her. He knew he'd have to approach her with caution. She might bolt or even scream. Given the insanity of the world, he'd probably end up trying to convince the crowd and then the cops that he wasn't a mugger or worse. So he followed her into the store at a discreet distance and asked himself what a bride on the run could possibly want in a Kmart?

Everything, it turned out.

Jessie grabbed a shopping cart and sailed down the aisles. Her cheeks glowed with color, so he knew she wasn't as oblivious to the gawkers as she tried to appear. She moved from counter to rack, snatching things only when there was a sale sign on view and dumping them into her cart. Jeans. A T-shirt. A desperately ugly lime-green nylon jacket whose claim to fame had to be the big sign that said not just Sale but Fifty Percent Off. She added a pair of sneakers to the stack, a tote bag, a toothbrush and things he'd always thought of as female survival gear.

Finally she headed for the register.

Liam hung back, observing her from behind a display that advertised a Blue Light Special on dinnerware. The clerk rang the items up, Jessie handed over a bill and got back only a couple of coins. Goodbye cheap motel room. He started forward as she scooped her packages from the cart, but she reversed direction so fast he almost stumbled as he scooted back behind the dinnerware.

When it was safe, he followed.

She led him straight to the rest rooms and disappeared into the ladies' lounge. He leaned against a counter a couple of aisles over, folded his arms, crossed his ankles, looked down at his feet like any other guy, bored as he waited for the missus. Obviously, she was going to change her clothes, but then what? Maybe Carrie was wrong, and she had more than fifty bucks.

The minutes dragged by. Jessie's followers wandered off. Liam shifted his weight, unfolded his arms, tucked his hands into the pockets of his jeans and planned his next move....

And then the door to the ladies' room opened, and all coherent thought flew away.

Bill Thornton's bride was gone. Proper, elegant Jessica had been replaced by Jessie, a woman ready to try anything, the quicksilver woman Liam had sensed was inside her from the beginning.

She'd stripped the roses from her hair and brushed it out so that it hung in honey-colored waves down her back. She was wearing the clothing he'd watched her buy, even the ugly lime-green jacket. But it didn't seem ugly now. As Liam looked at her, at that face scrubbed clean of makeup and artifice, he knew, with gut-wrenching certainty, that everything he'd been telling himself was a lie.

He wanted Jessie still, wanted her in a way that frightened him. When she lifted her head and saw him, she suddenly stiffened. But what he read in her eyes in that single, unguarded moment told him that she wanted him in exactly the same way.

She turned and ran.

Liam went after her, let her keep her lead through the store, through the parking lot, picking up his pace only when she neared her car. Then he caught her by the elbow and swung her toward him.

She swatted at him with both hands. "Let me go," she panted. "Damn you, Liam—"

"Jessie." He clasped her wrists, gripped them tightly, held her hands captive against his chest. "Jessie, listen to me."

"What for? Haven't you done enough?"

He hadn't. He'd only kissed her once, held her once, but that wasn't why he was here. He'd come after her for Bill. She belonged to Bill.

"Forget what happened," he said gruffly. "It's history."

"History?" She laughed. "We were climbing all over each other five minutes before I was supposed to say 'I do,' and you say that's history?" Angrily she jerked against his hands. "Maybe you can forget what we did, but I can't."

"Of course you can. Okay, we did something neither of us is proud of, but—"

"I'd never be able to look at William again without thinking of how I betrayed him."

"Dammit, we all make mistakes."

"Yes," she said coldly, "but not all of us are so callous that we can pretend they didn't happen."

Liam let go of her. "Bill wants you back."

"Well, I'm not going back."

"You have to! Otherwise—"

"Otherwise, what?" She smiled thinly. "You'll have to admit to your part in this mess?"

"This has nothing to do with me," Liam said quickly.

"Oh, give me a break." Jessie's eyes narrowed. "You're no better than I am. You decided to find me and fast-talk me into going back to William so you wouldn't have to live the rest of your life dodging the sight of yourself in mirrors." Her mouth twisted. "Spare me the lies, Liam. This has everything to do with you."

He stepped forward, his eyes hard and cold. "Okay. I'm not proud of what I did, but I'm not the one who decided to handle it by running away and leaving Bill at the altar."

Jessie's face fell. "Was he—was he very upset?"

"Was he…" Liam laughed. "Hell, no. The woman he loves leaves him a note and takes off just before she's supposed to become his wife. Why would he be upset?"

"I didn't want to hurt him," she whispered. "I'd have done anything—"

"Anything but go through with the wedding."

"How can you say that to me, damn you?" Her face lifted, and there was the glitter of tears in her eyes. "He's your friend. Do you really want him to marry a woman who—who was in another man's arms right before the ceremony?"

Not another man's, Liam thought. *My arms. Mine….*

"There's no point in ruining Bill's life because of a moment's stupidity," he said gruffly.

Jessie stared at him. Then she swung away and unlocked the door to her car. "And what about my life?" Her voice broke. "Did you ever think of that?"

"Dammit!" Liam grabbed her and turned her toward him. "You love him. You said so. What am I supposed to say, huh? 'Bill, look, maybe it's better all around if the wedding's off?'"

"Say whatever you like. Just—just don't break his heart by telling him the truth."

"Look, let's start again, okay? Bill asked me to find you, and to ask you to come back to him."

"Why didn't he come himself? Oh, don't bother answering. William knows you're a master at convincing women to do things they don't want to do."

"Fine. That's how you want to play it?" A muscle knotted in his jaw. "I'll take the responsibility. All of it, if that makes you feel better. What happened was my fault."

"It was! I certainly wouldn't have…" Jessie hesitated. "No. It wasn't. I wanted you to kiss me, Liam. I thought about what it would be like, all last night."

"Don't say that," Liam said quickly, trying not to think about the rush of pleasure he felt hearing her confession.

"Why shouldn't I? I can't tell William the truth, but I'm tired of lying to myself." Her voice wobbled again but her gaze was steady. "You're right. We made a mistake. Period. End of story—except that mistake made me face something I think I've known for weeks. I'm not right for William or maybe—maybe he's not right for me. Either way, I'm not going to marry him. Tell him I wish him all the best. Tell him…" Tears filled her eyes. "Oh, God," she whispered, "I'm so ashamed."

Liam didn't think. He reached out and Jessie went into his embrace as if she'd been born for no other reason.

He held her close, his face buried in her hair, his body

warmed by hers. She wept softly, her face in the hollow of his throat, and he whispered to her, words he'd never even thought to use with another woman, words of comfort, of solace, and gradually her tears lessened.

"Liam," she said, and he felt as if a hand were reaching into his chest and closing around his heart.

She pulled back in his arms and looked up at him. Her eyes were tear dampened and swollen. He kept one arm around her, dug in his jeans' pocket, took out a folded white handkerchief, dabbed at her eyes, then held it to her nose.

"Blow," he said gently. She smiled a little and did as he'd asked, and he laid his hand against her cheek, threaded his fingers into her hair and tilted her face to his.

"I can't marry William."

Liam wanted to tell her that she could, but the words caught in his throat. A woman wasn't supposed to weep like this on her wedding day. He'd already made one wrong judgment, thinking she was after Bill's name and money, and he'd be damned if he wanted to make another.

"He's a wonderful man. And I love him, but not the way I should. I didn't realize that, Liam. I swear I didn't."

He nodded. He knew that, too.

Jessie gave a shuddering sigh. "Tell him I'll be fine. He mustn't worry about me. And tell him I'll get in touch with him, once I—once I get my head together."

"Come back with me. Tell him yourself."

She shook her head and moved out of his arms. "I can't. Not yet. If I did he might realize…he might see…" She opened the door of her car and got behind the wheel. "Goodbye, Liam."

"No," he said, "Jessie, wait—"

She moved quickly, heard his hands slap against the car as she put it in gear, and then she was moving and he was running across the lot. Seconds later, a shiny black Corvette was on her tail and she choked back a spurt of hysterical laughter. What else would Liam Malone drive, except for a car that was sexy and fast?

She drove recklessly, tossing aside her usual caution, but his car followed hers like a shadow. A horn blared. Jessie looked to her left, saw a white-faced driver shake a fist at her. Chagrined, she realized she was endangering everybody on the road, and she slowed her car. There was no reason to drive so fast. What was she running from? Liam? That was ridiculous. He couldn't make her do anything she didn't want to do.

Yes, he can, a sly little voice whispered inside her head. *All he has to do is kiss you, and you're lost.*

No, she wasn't. She'd never been the kind of woman whose head could be turned by a handsome man.

Well, then, the voice said, even more slyly, *maybe you're running from yourself.*

That was even crazier. Just because she'd turned to jelly in Liam's arms, just because he was all the dangerous things Bill wasn't, things she'd spent her life trying to avoid....

She had a plan. Maybe it wasn't great. Still, without money or credit, she had only one place to go where she could marshal her thoughts, and one way to get there.

Liam was right behind her as she took the exit ramp, but it didn't matter. She'd left her groom, her wedding and her carefully planned life. Now she'd leave the man who'd made her realize that she didn't want any of those things. If she had, she'd never have been unfaithful to William and yes, that was what she'd been, unfaithful, kissing a stranger, wanting him, still wanting him....

Jessie swiped at her eyes with the back of her hand, drove into the airport and pulled into the first parking spot she saw. Liam did the same thing. He was behind her as she locked her door and started briskly toward the AmericAir terminal.

"Jessie!" His footsteps pounded after her. "Jessie!"

He caught up to her, clasped her arm. She wrenched it free.

"Leave me alone, Liam."

"Do you think I'm just going to let you run away? We have to talk."

The terminal doors slid open. She stepped inside, walked to a departure board, checked it. If she remembered correctly, there'd been a morning flight to Miami as well as the one she and William had planned to take. Yes, there it was, Flight 937, leaving from gate twelve. With luck, she could swap her ticket and get on this plane. But there wasn't much time. She picked up her pace, almost stumbled when Liam did a quick two-step to get in front of her.

"You can't solve anything by running away from it."

She moved around him, dumped her tote bag on the conveyor belt at the security checkpoint and went through the gate with Liam right behind her. When she heard the buzzer go off, she heaved a sigh of relief.

Goodbye, Liam, she thought, and blinked back the tears that welled in her eyes again.

"Sir?" said a polite voice. "Would you empty your pockets, please?"

Liam bit back a groan, dumped his change into a receptacle and watched as Jessie merged with the crowd. By the time he started after her, she'd disappeared. He moved quickly from one gate to the next. She could be anywhere by now. If only he had some idea...

There she was, at the information desk at gate twelve. Liam looked at the sign behind the desk. Flight 937 to Miami, it said. Departing at 10:45. He looked at his watch. It was 10:15. Not that it mattered. Jessie wasn't going anywhere, not without a ticket. But she was. Everything clicked into place. No cash, no credit card needed, not if she'd made all her arrangements via the Internet. With luck, she could even switch to an earlier departure.

"Where are you guys going on your honeymoon?" he'd asked last night, as he'd tried to make conversation and get his mind off Bill's fiancée.

"Florida," Bill had replied with a quick smile at Jessie. "Hibiscus Key. Well—" he'd blushed "—actually, it's a place called Couples' Cove." He'd looped his arm lightly around Jessie's shoulders. "Jessica made the arrangements. She makes all my travel plans on the computer, don't you, dear?"

And Jessie had torn her eyes from Liam, cleared her throat and said yes, yes, she did, and they'd continued with some meaningless chitchat.

Liam swung away and ran through the terminal to the

AmericAir ticket counter while he dug his cell phone from his pocket. There were two people ahead of him. "Emergency," he said, and stepped quickly to the head of the line as he punched in Bill's number.

"Hello?"

It was Carrie's voice. "Put Bill on," Liam said curtly.

"He's resting. I hate to wake him, Mr. Malone. He's had such a bad—"

"Give him a message. Tell him…" He looked up. The ticket clerk was staring at him, eyebrows raised. "Hang on," he said, and hit the mute button. "One seat, Flight 937 to Miami." He dug in his pocket, took out his driver's license and his credit card, handed them over. "Charge the ticket, and there's my photo ID."

"Coach or first class?"

"First class. Look, pal, the flight's going to be boarding in—"

"It's already boarding, sir. If fact, I don't know if I can—"

"Just do it," Liam said tersely, and put the phone to his ear. "Carrie? Tell Bill… Tell him I…" Liam watched as the clerk began typing his ticket. Jessie was on that plane. She was leaving Seattle, putting three thousand miles between them. "Tell him that I've found Jessie. She's at the airport, and she's fine, and—" And what? "Tell him I'll be in touch," he said, and hit the disconnect button as the clerk handed him his ticket.

The attendant was just closing the door that led to the boarding ramp as Liam sprinted through the gate. "Wait," he yelled. "That's my flight."

The attendant opened the door and reached for the phone. "Talk about cutting it close—"

He thundered down the ramp to the plane. The flight attendant greeted him with a smile.

"Just about missed it," she said brightly.

He nodded, struggled to catch his breath. "Yeah," he said—and then he saw Jessie, sitting by the window, alone in the last row of the first-class cabin. She looked up and saw him, and for the first time in his life, Liam knew what people meant when they said they were terrified, because that was how he felt now, scared right through to the marrow of his bones.

His eyes never left hers as he walked down the aisle. "I almost missed the flight," he said softly when he reached her. "I probably could have bluffed my way into picking up Bill's ticket and using it, but I didn't want to."

Jessie touched the tip of her tongue to her bottom lip. "Why not?"

"Because I'm not standing in for Bill, or speaking for him. Not anymore. Do you understand that?"

Her mouth trembled as Liam sat down and took her hand. "Yes," she whispered. "Oh, yes, I understand."

Liam took Jessie's face in his hands. This time, when their lips met, it was in a kiss so tender that it almost turned him inside out.

CHAPTER FOUR

THE SEAT BELT SIGN BLINKED OFF when the plane reached cruising altitude.

Liam looked at Jessie. The softness of her smile, the undisguised joy with which she'd greeted him, were gone. Instead, she stared straight ahead, features rigid, face pale, her hand turning to ice in his.

"Jessie," he said, and she looked at him, her eyes wide with a fear he could only guess at.

He wanted to gather her into his embrace. He'd always liked having a woman in his arms, in bed or on a dance floor, but women in need of soothing made him feel clumsy. That wasn't how he felt now. He wanted to hold her, not to kiss her but to comfort her, warm her, rock her against him as if she'd just awakened from a bad dream and only he could chase away the demons.

"It's a long flight," he said to ease the tension.

She gave him a strained smile. "I know. Almost five and a half hours."

Liam cleared his throat. "How about some wine? Or some coffee? I can ask the flight attendant to—"

"No, I'm fine."

She wasn't. The shadows under her eyes looked like bruises and he fought back the desire to press his mouth to that tender skin, to draw her close.

"Well," he said briskly, "I think I'm going to read for a while." He let go of her hand and fumbled in the pocket of the seat in front of him. "Sometimes these airline magazines are pretty interesting."

Airline magazines were interesting? He was running away with his best friend's fiancée, he ached with the need to make love to her, and now he was going to bury his nose in a magazine?

Damn right, he was. Otherwise, he was going to take her in his arms and say things he didn't believe in, things he'd never imagined ever saying to any woman, much less one who belonged to Bill.

"Let me know if you need anything," he said, as brightly as a waiter hoping for a big tip. Then he whipped open the magazine and pretended that the print wasn't one enormous gray blur.

JESSIE STARED OUT HER WINDOW.

Liam was reading. Reading, she thought, and clamped her lips together so hard her jaw hurt. He'd turned her life inside out, made her run away from her wedding, followed her through half of Seattle and onto a plane headed for the other side of the continent, and now he was sitting next to her, engrossed in a stupid magazine.

It was hard to know who she despised more, herself for letting him ruin her life or him for doing it.

"Excuse me," she said coldly, and shot to her feet. Liam looked up, his brows lifted as if he'd never seen her before. "I have to go to the bathroom," she said, even more coldly, and he rose so she could march past him. It seemed like a good move, but it turned out that her timing was rotten. She was halfway up the aisle when a man in the first row stood up and went into the lavatory.

Jessie blew out a breath, folded her arms and leaned back against the bulkhead. Perfect. He was the only other passenger in first class, and he'd made it to the bathroom ahead of her. Well, why not? The entire morning had been perfect, starting with the moment she'd been stupid enough to think she didn't want to go through with the wedding, stupid enough to think the rush of lust Liam Malone had stirred in her blood was anywhere near as important as the love she felt for William. As for what she'd felt when she saw Liam board the plane—what she'd thought she'd felt—that had been nothing but surprise.

She glanced at her watch, frowned and looked balefully at the Occupied sign on the lavatory door. What was taking so long? Airplane bathrooms were little more than high-tech closets, first class or not. She wanted to splash some cold water in her eyes, think about the best way to tell Liam that she'd changed her mind, thank you very much, but she wasn't going to Hibiscus Key with him.

Did he really think she'd let him take William's place in their honeymoon bed?

The door to the lavatory opened. The man who'd been inside stepped out. He smiled. Jessie glared and moved into the narrow space. The guy's cologne engulfed her.

William wore cologne, too. She'd thought she'd liked the smell—it seemed masculine and fresh—until Liam had taken her in his arms. He didn't seem to wear any cologne at all. He smelled of things she couldn't quite put her finger on. Soap, maybe, and fresh air and leather. And of himself. Pure male, intriguing, sexy…

"Oh, stop it," she said through her teeth.

Scowling, she locked the door, then met her reflection in the mirror. It wasn't a happy moment. The lime-green jacket had been cheap, but it was ugly as sin. The rest of her wasn't much better. Brushing the gel from her hair had left it an unruly mess. Her face was as shiny as a polished apple. Her nose was pink, her eyelids swollen. How Liam could still want her was…

Not that it mattered.

Her scowl deepened as she turned on the water, scooped it onto her face, then dried off with a towel. Who cared what she looked like, or whether or not Liam wanted her? She'd been crazy to run, crazy to think she wanted him, crazy to—

There was a tap at the lavatory door. What was with people, anyway? Occupied meant exactly that.

The tap came again.

"Just a minute," she said irritably. She balled up the towel, dumped it, took a deep breath and undid the bolt.

Liam stepped inside the narrow little room. Jessie stumbled back as he shut and locked the door.

"Are you crazy? Liam, dammit, what are you doing? You can't—"

"Just shut up," he snapped, "just shut the hell—" His

arms went around her and his mouth came down, hard, on hers.

He *was* crazy. And so was she, because the instant she felt his lips on hers, she moaned, threw her arms around his neck and kissed him back. He groaned, spread his hands over her hips, pulled her against him and slid his tongue into her mouth. Jessie whimpered, arched against him and he whispered her name, slid his hands inside her jacket, under her T-shirt, and cupped her breasts. She fell back against the sink as he ran his thumbs over her nipples.

"Liam. Oh, Liam."

For one wild, wonderful moment, they were lost in passion. Then Liam tore his mouth from Jessie's, put his hands on her waist and leaned his forehead against hers.

No way was he going to take her like this. Not the first time. He wasn't even sure how he'd gotten into the lavatory. He certainly hadn't planned it. One minute he'd been sitting there, telling himself he really was interested in reading a review of a new Miami restaurant and the next, he'd looked up, asked himself why he was acting as if he was on an unimportant flight when he knew, dammit, knew, that this was the most important flight of his life. He'd shot to his feet and headed for the locked door and the woman behind it without really knowing why he was going after her or what he'd do when he got there. But when she opened the door, he knew he was there to hold her and taste her and remind them both that what had started in that garden was too powerful to deny.

She was looking at him now, a smile trembling on her

mouth, and he sensed, without having to ask, that her anger had come from the same place as his fake disinterest. He sensed, too, that whatever was happening between them had never happened before, not to any man or woman on the planet.

"Jessie."

Her smile broadened. It lit her face, even her eyes, and he felt his lips curve in response.

"Liam?"

"I know what you're thinking."

She laughed. She blushed, too, and he realized he'd never seen a woman blush before, not quite like that, as if she really meant it.

"I know what you're thinking, too," she said.

Hell, she was really something. He wanted to kiss her again but he knew it would be a mistake. It was difficult enough to just stand here without taking her in his arms and finishing what they'd started.

"I didn't mean that." He grinned and stepped back the inch the cramped space permitted. "I mean, yeah, that's what I'm thinking, but—" he took a deep breath "—you're thinking you did the wrong thing."

Her smile faded. "Yes."

"That you shouldn't have run away."

"Maybe," she said in a little whisper.

"You're thinking you know Bill and you don't know a damn thing about me, and that you've never done anything so crazy in your life."

He saw her try to smile again, but she couldn't quite pull it off. "Yes and yes," she said, her eyes lifting to his.

"Well, neither have I." He reached out, tucked her hair behind her ears, smoothed down the collar of her lime-green jacket. Then he looped his hands loosely behind her neck and leaned his forehead against hers again. "I've never run away with a woman."

"Never?"

Liam shook his head. "I've done a lot of things on impulse, but nothing like this."

"I thought—I mean…" She licked her lips. "William always talks about how—how successful you are with women. And I just figured—"

"That I swoop in, snatch one, and carry her off when the mood's on me?" This time, she really did smile and he kissed her gently, capturing her only with the kiss. "This is a first for me," he said softly. "I wanted you to know that."

She nodded. "Thank you for telling me."

Her tone was solemn. Liam took the edges of her jacket and drew her close. "You're welcome," he said, just as solemnly. "You should know another thing, too." He looked into her eyes. "We're not going to Hibiscus Key."

"We're not?"

He shook his head. "I know a place off the Florida coast. Flamingo Island. It's beautiful. White sand beaches, bright emerald water, soft blue sky, privacy so complete you'll think we've gone back to the Garden of Eden and that we're Adam and Eve."

"Ah," Jessie said with a smile she hoped didn't show what she was feeling. "A personal recommendation from Adam himself."

Liam had been there, all right. He thought of explaining how and why, decided this wasn't the time, and shook his head. "Only on business, sweetheart. Never with a woman."

"I didn't ask."

"You didn't have to." He framed her face in his hands, lifted it to him. "Everything about the next few days is going to be a first, Jess. For you, for me…for us."

The next few days. Well, he'd told her what he expected and she had to admire him for his honesty. William had offered forever, but that had been love. This was lust. She knew it, Liam knew it, and it was silly to pretend it was anything else.

"Jessie? Will you go there with me?"

She lifted her head and in that terrible, wonderful moment when their eyes met, she knew that she'd go anywhere with him, if he asked, that she would stay with him, if he asked.

"That sounds…" She smiled. "It sounds wonderful."

Liam kissed her. Then he unlocked the lavatory door and stepped into the cabin.

"The coast's clear," he whispered.

It was true. Nobody was watching them. The flight attendant wasn't in sight, and the man in the front row was sound asleep. Still, Jessie didn't take an easy breath until she was seated beside Liam again, safe in the protective curve of his arm. He drew a blanket over them, tucked it in and brought her head to his shoulder. It felt as if they were in a cocoon, with the rest of the world locked away.

"Close your eyes," he said. "See if you can get some rest."

She nodded and burrowed closer. She was exhausted, but she was too wired to sleep. So much had happened. She'd done things she'd never have believed herself capable of doing. Her life seemed to be spinning out of control and she still couldn't decide if that was terrifying or exhilarating. All she knew was that she'd never felt more alive than she did now. And she felt safe with Liam's arm around her, but how could that be? Nothing about him was safe. He was everything she'd avoided, everything she'd been afraid to want.

Maybe there were times it was best not to think too much about what you were doing.

Maybe this was one of those times.

NIGHT HAD FALLEN by the time they landed in Miami.

Liam told her he'd made some calls while she slept. Everything was ready for them, he said, holding her hand as he led her through the terminal.

She caught people looking at them. Why wouldn't they? Liam was so handsome. *Gorgeous* was the word. And she was probably glowing with excitement. It was hard to remember how frightened she'd been a few hours ago. She gave a soft laugh, and Liam looked at her and smiled.

"What?"

"Nothing. I just—I can't believe this is me. I mean, I never…" Jessie hesitated. "It's awful, isn't it? That this feels so right when William—"

"Don't think about Bill," Liam said quickly. "Not tonight."

He was right, Jessie told herself as she waited near the cash register in a brightly lit terminal gift shop. "I need some stuff," Liam had told her, and she'd nodded, knowing he meant things like a toothbrush, knowing he'd probably also meant condoms, but trying her best not to think about it. Not that she didn't want him to buy condoms. She was glad he saw that as his responsibility. The problem was, she could feel her nerves starting to take over again, feel the anticipation giving way to wariness.

Any second now, she half expected her conscience would demand to know if she had any idea at all of what she was doing.

She did. And she was going to do it anyway.

Liam caught her eye and smiled as he headed for the register. She smiled back, tried not to think about the condoms, looked down at the counter and the cheap souvenirs arrayed on it. She picked up a plastic alligator boasting a mouthful of teeth and an articulated tail, toyed with it, put it down, picked up a small plastic globe that held a bright green palm tree standing on white sand, set against a tropical cardboard sea. She tilted the globe and the sand turned the placid scene into a hurricane.

"Would you like that?" Liam said, and she looked up to find him standing close beside her.

"No." She gave a little laugh, put the globe down. "I mean, it's just silly, but…" Her voice trailed off. "Well," she said briskly, "did you get everything you needed?" Color flew into her cheeks. "I mean—"

"Everything I need, for now," he said easily. "There are

shops at the place we're going to. We can take care of the rest tomorrow."

"Fine," she said, even more briskly. "I won't be able to pay you back until after I return to—until I can get to my bank again."

"Jess."

"Hmm?"

"What's the matter?"

"Nothing. Why would you think—"

Liam picked up the little plastic globe. "You were looking at this thing as if it were a crystal ball."

"Was I?" She tried to smile, didn't quite make it and shrugged her shoulders instead. "It's just weird, that's all. I mean, one minute, the scene inside is so peaceful. Then you just give it a little tilt and it's as if this storm comes along and sweeps everything away." To her horror, her voice suddenly quavered. "It's frightening. That the world can tilt and your whole life can change in the blink of an eye."

"Let the world tilt," Liam said softly. He put his arm around her, drew her against his side. "I promise, I'll keep you safe."

THE PLANE THAT AWAITED THEM was small, and they were the only passengers. It lifted into a black sky hung with a huge ivory moon. Ivory, like the color of her wedding gown, Jessie thought, and shivered.

Liam shrugged off his leather jacket and draped it around her shoulders. He put his lips to her ear so she'd hear him over the roar of the engine. "Cold?"

"A little." She hesitated, then put her mouth to his ear. "How far is it to—what did you call this place?"

Her breath tickled his skin, her fragrance rose to his nostrils. Liam closed his eyes, told himself to take a couple of deep breaths when what he really wanted was to take a fistful of her hair and bury his face in it. But that would only make her more skittish than she already was. Jessie was vibrating like a tuning fork and only an idiot wouldn't have realized that she was having second and third and fourth thoughts. The last thing he wanted to do was rush her, or let her see how much trouble he was having hanging on to his self-control. He never lost control. Never. And that was all he'd done today, all he'd done since last night.

He sat up straight and cleared his throat.

"Flamingo Island," he said calmly. "I'll let you know when it comes into view."

When he did, Jessie looked out the window. All she could see was a glow in an otherwise inky sea. The plane circled, began its descent, touched down lightly. Liam thanked the pilot, climbed out, helped her down and led her to a canopied Jeep waiting in the short grass alongside the runway. The driver greeted him by name as they climbed into the back seat, and they set off.

"You won't be able to see much in the dark," Liam said, putting his arm around her shoulders. "I'll take you for a tour tomorrow. Okay?"

"Fine," she said, and she'd have laughed if she hadn't been afraid the laugh would turn into a sob. What was she doing here, in the middle of nowhere, with a man she didn't know? With her entire life, her oh-so-safe life, a million miles away?

The driver said something about the weather. Liam answered. Jessie just sat there, taking deep breaths and planning how and when to tell Liam she'd changed her mind again because she surely had. She wasn't going to stay on Flamingo Island and she certainly wasn't going to sleep with him.

Not that he'd said anything about sleeping.

Carefully, as if he might not notice, she eased free of his encircling arm.

They were traveling a road that skirted the water. She could hear the boom of the surf, smell the salt tang, but Liam had been right when he'd said she wouldn't be able to see much. Jessie bit her lip. Actually, all she wanted to see was the desk clerk, so she could find out how to arrange for a flight back to the mainland.

Finally the Jeep slowed. Several small buildings, and then a much larger one, blazing with lights, were just ahead.

Thank God, she thought—but the driver didn't stop. Jessie craned her neck and looked over her shoulder. "Wasn't that…" She licked her dry lips. "Wasn't that the hotel?"

"That was the main building, yes. But we have a private villa."

A private villa. She was still processing that when the Jeep bounced to a stop. Liam leaned forward, exchanged soft words with the driver. The man handed over a key; Liam handed over a tip and helped her from the Jeep.

From the effusiveness of the driver's thanks, she knew it was a large tip. She'd been right, then, when she'd figured that his luck had been good lately. That was the way it went for men like Liam Malone. Good luck, followed by bad luck. One woman, followed by another.

She spun toward the Jeep. "Wait," she started to say, but she was too late. The vehicle was roaring away.

"Jessie?"

Liam held out his hand. She hesitated, took it, and he led her up a narrow path of crushed white shells toward a villa that rose like a block of white sugar in the moonlight. She hung back as he opened the door and switched on the light.

Jessie caught her breath.

The villa was one enormous bedroom. White tile floors. Soaring white walls. Wood ceiling fans, blades turning lazily. A wall of glass looking out on a white beach. And a bed. An enormous four-poster bed mounted on a low platform like something out of a stage set, and draped in yards and yards of gauzy white lace.

Liam had brought her to a lover's paradise. Long, hot days in the sun. Longer, hotter nights in that bed. She felt as if a cold hand had wrapped around her heart. They weren't lovers, she and Liam Malone. They were a man and a woman brought to this place by lust, and once they'd sated their hunger, they'd go their separate ways. She'd understood that.

Except, she couldn't go through with it.

She took a quick step back. "I can't," she said. "I can't do this."

Liam shut the door, leaned back against it and folded his arms. "And just when, exactly, did you reach that decision?"

His tone was polite, his expression pleasant. But there was something just under his words, something flickering in his eyes, that made her shiver.

"Does it matter? I only know that—that—"

"That you can't do this." A muscle knotted in his jaw. "Is that how you ended up saying yes to Bill when he asked you to marry him?"

Her head came up. "What?"

"You heard me. Is that how it happened? Did you lie to yourself about your feelings, tell yourself you loved him when you knew that you didn't?"

Jessie stood straighter. She dropped the tote bag and put her hands on her hips. "I never lied to William."

A tight smile etched Liam's mouth. "I didn't accuse you of lying to him. I asked if you'd lied to yourself."

"That's ridiculous. Lie to myself? About my feelings?"

She tossed her head and the spill of her hair over her shoulders was like the swirl of a flamenco dancer's skirt. Liam unfolded his arms and dug his hands into his pockets. It didn't matter that she was beautiful, that he wanted her more than he'd ever wanted a woman in his life or that he could seduce her in a moment because, even if she wasn't ready to admit it, her need for him was as wild as his for her. What mattered was that she come to him on her own, that she put aside the lies and give herself to him fully. That was how he wanted her; it was the only way he wanted her. It was the way she wanted him, too, and he needed to hear her say it.

"Why would I lie? William's a wonderful man."

"You don't love him."

"He has so many wonderful qualities that I could never list them all."

"And you still don't love him."

"He's kind and good and decent, and he'd never, not in a thousand lifetimes, do what you've done."

"No, he wouldn't." Liam narrowed his eyes and stepped away from the door. "That's the difference between us, I guess. I see what I want and I take it."

Jessie's skin prickled. "Charming. I bet that goes over big with the ladies."

"Maybe I should clarify that." He reached behind him, turned the lock, then came toward her as lithely as a big cat, his green eyes locked to hers. "I only take what's offered to me. I'm honest in what I want, Jessie. I don't lie to a woman."

"That's even better," she said, and hoped he couldn't see the pulse leaping in the hollow of her throat. "Really a smooth come-on, Liam. You telling a woman you know what she really wants, even when she says you're wrong."

He reached out, cupped her shoulders with his hands. "Don't do this. If you don't want to be with me, say so. But, dammit, don't play games. Not now."

"I don't want to be with you. Okay? Is that what you wanted to hear?"

"I want to hear the truth." His eyes were dark and angry. She felt the press of his fingers, knew the tension that was building inside him because it was inside her, too. "Say it. Say that you want me."

"You've no idea what I want, Liam. You—"

He kissed her. Not hard. She'd have fought him, if he had. He kissed her gently, his mouth moving lightly over hers.

"Say it," he whispered. "Let the world tilt, sweetheart. Let it happen."

Jessie's heart thudded. How could he know her so well when he hardly knew her at all? He brought her hands to his chest. She could feel his heart racing under her fingers. A honeyed weakness was spreading through her bones. It would be so easy to do...

"Let go," she said sharply. "Damn you, let go of me!"

He did, so suddenly that she stumbled back. "To hell with it," he growled.

"Oh, that's nice." Her voice trembled. She grabbed her bag and stepped around him, heading for the door. "You can't get what you want so you say to hell with it?"

"*You're* the one who's not getting what you want, because I'm not about to deliver."

"What are you talking about?"

Liam grabbed her again and backed her against the wall. "You're a coward, Jessie. You're so afraid of behaving like a real woman that you want me to do it all. What did you have in mind, huh? Am I supposed to turn into a villain? Maybe you'd like me to play at being some kind of Don Juan, a guy who can talk a woman into bed even if she keeps saying she doesn't want to be there." He let go of her. "Well, I won't do it. You cast the wrong guy in the part."

Her hand whirred through the air and cracked across

his cheek. His head snapped back; he cursed and grabbed her wrist before she could hit him again…and then she was in his arms, her mouth pressed hungrily to his, her fingers knotting in his sweatshirt as his fingers tangled in her hair.

"Jessie." He caught hold of her face and brushed her mouth with his. "Sweetheart, I'm sorry. I didn't mean—"

"It was my fault. I was afraid, Liam. Not of you," she added quickly. "Never of you. I was afraid of the way you make me feel."

The look on his face made her breath catch. He swept his hand down her back, lifting her into him, watching her eyes darken as he pressed against her.

"Tell me how I make you feel," he said thickly.

"As if…" Her jacket fell to the floor and his hands, his hard, exciting hands, slid under her T-shirt and over her skin. When he cupped her breasts, her voice broke. "As if—Liam. Make love to me. Please, please, pl—"

Liam kissed her, swept her into his arms and carried her to the bed.

CHAPTER FIVE

WHAT HAD STARTED in the garden would end here. They'd known each other for little more than twenty-four hours. Still, as Liam drew Jessie to him, he felt as if he'd waited all his life to make love to her. He wanted to tell her that, but she reached her arms up to him and sighed his name, and words became meaningless.

All that mattered was touch. And taste. And scent.

He kissed her gently, moving his lips over hers, waiting for her mouth to soften and cling to his. When it did, he slipped his tongue between her lips, groaning with pleasure at the honeyed sweetness he found waiting for him. Her arms tightened around him, her body arched against his, and he rolled her beneath him, caught her bottom lip between his teeth and eased the small hurt with a kiss. Jessie moaned softly, and the need to take her pounded through his blood.

Slow down, he told himself, slow down. He'd been a gambler most of his life and understood that when you bet on the toss of the dice, you put your money on today. Only a fool would bet on tomorrow, or think that far ahead.

Right now the wheel of fortune had spun and the little red ball with his number on it had dropped into the slot. That was all he'd count on but, if he was very lucky, he could make the moment last.

He tunneled his hands into her hair and swept it back from her face. He kissed her temples, her eyelids, her throat as she arched against him again. Lord, she was beautiful, especially now, as the wildness he'd sensed in her from the beginning burst free. Little sounds were breaking from her throat; the musk of arousal rose from her skin. Such silky skin. Such hot, golden skin.

"Liam," she whispered, and kissed him, her mouth taking his mouth, her breath mingling with his breath. She slid her hands under his shirt, laid them against his chest. His body clenched like a fist. Slow down, he told himself again, slow down....

And then he stopped thinking.

He grasped the hem of her T-shirt and tried to pull it up, but the thin cotton tore apart in his hands, exposing her to him. She wore a sheer bra, the color of her skin. No lace, no silk, bows or ribbons, nothing but the lush round-ness of her breasts and the tawny satin of her nipples.

The room swam out of focus. He bent to her, smoothed the tip of his finger over her breasts, kissed them, licked them. Jessie cried out, moaned his name as he kissed her and swallowed her cries.

He reached for the front clasp of her bra. Her hands, cold as ice, locked on his wrists.

"Wait," she said shakily. "Liam, please wait."

His body told him to ignore her plea. His mind, or

maybe his heart, said something different. *I'm afraid of what you make me feel,* she'd said, and he'd reacted by ripping her clothes off.

He groaned, rolled over and threw his arm across his eyes. "Jessie," he said when he could trust himself to talk. "Sweetheart…"

He reached out to her but she moved quickly, clutched the blanket around her and stood up, facing away from him. "I'm sorry," she said stiffly. "I know you're disappointed."

Liam got to his feet. Gently he peeled the blanket from her hands and dropped it to the floor. "Jessie," he said again, and drew her back against him. Her body was rigid against his; he knew she wanted him to let go. Instead, he put his arms around her waist. "I'm the one who's sorry, Jessie. Can you forgive me?"

"There's nothing to—"

"There is." He turned her in his arms, stroked her back, pressed kisses into her hair. "I came at you with all the finesse of a sex-starved water buffalo."

She made a little sound, half sob, half laugh, against his shoulder. "How do you know how a sex-starved water buffalo would behave?"

Liam smiled. "It's something about males, I guess. Show us a beautiful female, we lose our cool." His voice roughened. "Especially if she touches some special place inside us."

Jessie lifted her head, leaned back in his arms. "Have I?" she whispered. "Touched something special inside you? Because—because that's how I feel about you, as if you've reached into me and—and…" She sighed and buried her face against him again. "And that's crazy. We don't even know each other."

"We will, though. I promise." Gently he scooped her into his arms. She looped her arms around his neck and sighed.

"You must think I'm an idiot."

"What I think," Liam replied as he made his way across the room, "is that we've damn near broken the how-long-can-a-human-being-stay-awake record." Jessie laughed. It was a real laugh this time, a wonderful sound, and Liam grinned at her. "You like that, huh?"

"You made it up. There is no such record."

"Well, if there isn't, there should be." He kissed her, then jabbed the light switch with his elbow. Velvet darkness swallowed the room. "Okay," he said briskly, "here's the plan."

"The plan?" Jessie swallowed. Liam was heading back toward the bed, washed in ivory moonlight. "Liam?" She hesitated. "I think you should know…I mean, if you think it's the light—if you think turning it off will—"

"I know that, sweetheart."

He laid her on the bed and stood over her. She caught her breath as he pulled off his sweatshirt. He was beautiful. The hard, masculine face. The broad shoulders. The wide chest and narrow waist.

"What I thought," he said huskily, "was that we'd get some sleep."

"I won't be able to sleep," she said quickly. "I'm too—too—"

"Let's try, anyway." She heard the thud of his sneakers as he kicked them off. His hands went to his waist and he opened his belt, undid his zipper. The denim rustled as he stepped out of his jeans and stood before her, clad only in a pair of dark boxer shorts slung low on his hips. "The thing is, I can't sleep with the light on." A smile curved his lips. "Or with most of my clothes on, either." The mattress dipped gently as he sat down beside her. Jessie could hear her blood beating in her ears.

"Liam," she whispered.

"Shh." He took her hands, brought them to his chest, and she caught her breath at the feel of hot skin, tight muscle, silky hair. "That's not so awful, is it?"

No. Oh, no, it wasn't. It was wonderful touching him. He was so alive, so real, so excitingly male.

His fingers were at the front clasp of her bra. This time she didn't stop him. A languid heat was moving through her body. She could almost feel herself turning to liquid. When the clasp gave way, he drew the bra off and tossed it aside.

"I want to feel your skin against mine," he said. "That's all, I promise. Is that all right, Jessie?"

She didn't answer. She couldn't, but Liam seemed to understand her silence. He put his arms around her and when her naked flesh touched his, she caught her breath. He lowered his head to hers and kissed her. Desire, sharp and hot, began to boil in her blood.

"Let's just get you out of some of this stuff."

She sighed her acquiescence, sat up so he could undress her. When she had nothing on but her panties, he eased her back against the pillows and kissed her mouth, her throat, her shoulders. She closed her eyes and waited, her skin tingling, for the feel of his lips on her breasts.

This was what she'd dreamed of last night. This slow, scalding seduction. Liam in her arms. A burning ache, low in her belly. When he finally stretched out beside her, she turned toward him, trembling, every breath searing her lungs.

"Liam," she whispered. "Liam—"

He put two fingers lightly over her lips, drew the blanket over them. Then he gathered her into the strength of his embrace.

She almost came apart at the first touch of his body against hers, the first awareness of his erection pressed against her belly. She waited for him to move against her, to strip away the last flimsy barriers that separated them, yearned for it to happen.

"Go to sleep, darling," he whispered.

He stroked her back, kissed her temple. After a while, his breathing slowed. So did hers, but she knew it was meaningless. He was pretending and so was she. Neither of them would get any sleep, not pressed together like this, with their hearts beating in unison, her breasts against his chest. Nevertheless, his heartbeat steadied. Hers did, too.

He really had fallen asleep, she thought in surprise.

Moments later, so did she.

LIAM CAME AWAKE SLOWLY.

It was just before dawn. A pale pewter light was seeping into the room, and Jessie was still in his arms. She was asleep, cradled against him, and he fought back the desire to dip his head and awaken her with a kiss.

Only when she was ready. Not until then.

He put out his hand and smoothed a silken tangle of honey-gold hair back from her cheek.

The amazing thing was, he'd made it through the night. A smile angled across his mouth. What he'd pretty much figured was that lying with a half-naked Jessie in his arms would kill him. The first touch of her skin against his had almost been his undoing. He'd told himself to lie still, slow his breathing, convince her he was asleep. It must have worked because, eventually, she'd sighed and relaxed against him.

Holding her, keeping her safe through the night, wasn't much of a price to pay for having her come to him without fear or hesitation.

The funny thing was that he'd never much liked to spend the night with a woman. Not that he was a guy who was into wham, bam, thank you, ma'am. He always held a woman after sex, shared her bed for an hour or two before getting up and heading home. If a woman asked him to stay the night, and most did, he said he was a restless sleeper. It wasn't a lie. He almost always awakened sprawled across the bed, the blankets off and the pillows on the floor.

Liam drew Jessie closer.

This time, though, he'd awakened just the way he'd gone to sleep, lying in the center of the big bed, Jessie in his embrace, her head on his shoulder. Sometime during the night, she'd put her hand on his chest. It lay just over his heart. He'd moved a little, too. He'd thrown his leg over hers in what any shrink would surely have defined as a subconscious gesture meant to keep her with him.

Strange behavior for a man who preferred to sleep alone.

Maybe the simple truth was that sleeping alone wasn't as important as waking up alone. Maybe he just didn't want to greet the day with a stranger beside him, even if she wasn't actually a stranger. He'd never been into one-night stands. The thing was, no matter how hot the affair, a man and a woman were forever separate entities, and making love to a woman was less intimate than sleeping alongside her. It might sound crazy, but it had always seemed logical—until now. He'd just slept beside Jessie, they hadn't even made love, and he'd known her for all of—Liam lifted his arm, squinted at his watch. For all of thirty-something hours.

Thirty-something hours, and in all that time he'd phoned Bill exactly once and left a message that told him nothing. But then, how did you go about telling a man who was crazy with worry that he had nothing to worry about, because you'd not just found his bride, you'd run off with her?

Liam eased his arm from beneath Jessie's shoulders and sat up. He took one last look at her, then pulled on his jeans and made his way to a small alcove near the patio where a rattan cabinet hid a minifridge, a stocked wine rack and an electric coffeemaker, ready to go.

He turned the coffeemaker on. That was one of the first things he'd changed when he bought Flamingo Island Resort.

"We don't provide any food or drink in the villas," the manager had told him with an officious little smile. "Most of our guests are honeymooners. They don't want to be bothered with such things."

Liam knew the officious smile probably was the result of the rumor that said he'd won the place in a game of poker. So he'd smiled pleasantly and pointed out that that was precisely the reason the resort would provide champagne, wine, coffee and tea, plus a basket of fresh-baked breads to be left on each porch in the morning.

"And by the way," he'd added with a smile that was more than a match for the manager's, "just so we understand each other, Mr. Edding, I didn't win this place playing cards."

Edding had paled. "No, sir. I never said—"

"Be sure you don't."

They'd gotten along just fine after that.

Liam took a bright red mug from the cabinet and filled it with hot coffee.

Two years had gone by since that day. Flamingo Island, always successful, had become a world-class resort. Liam had added two more properties to the string, and hadn't played so much as a hand of poker in all that time. It had taken a while, but he'd finally figured out that a man couldn't go through life gambling on everything.

Until he'd stood in the departure terminal at Sea-Tac Airport and decided to bet his honor against his need for a woman he knew he couldn't have.

The hot tropical sun was rising over the ocean, turning the water to shimmering gold as he stepped out onto the patio. He sipped at his coffee, leaned his elbows on the sea wall and tried to figure out what to do next. A man of principle would call Bill and tell him everything. Good Lord, how could he do that? What was "everything," anyway? What would he say? "Bill, I don't know how to tell you this, but Jessie and I are together. We're in our own private world, and she won't be coming back to Seattle for a while."

"Liam?"

He turned around. Jessie was standing in the doorway. She'd pulled on his sweatshirt but not her jeans. Her hair was a confusion of honey-gold waves. Her eyes were bright as the ocean, her skin as flushed as the morning sky, and he knew, in that moment, that he was never going to let her leave him.

"I thought I smelled coffee," she said with a hesitant smile. "Liam? About last night—"

He was beside her before she'd finished the sentence. He swung her into his arms, kissed her, and she put her arms around his neck.

"I wasn't ready last night," she whispered. "But I am now."

Liam carried her inside, lay down with her in his arms. He rolled her onto her belly, drew her hair away from her neck and pressed his lips to her skin. The scent of her rose to his nostrils, a delicious blend of flowers, salt air, and woman. Gently he eased up the sweatshirt, eased down her panties. He heard her catch her breath as he kissed the long curve of her spine, the dimple at its base before turning her over.

"You're beautiful," he said huskily, his eyes locked to hers.

She smiled. "You are, too."

He laughed softly. "Men aren't beautiful, sweetheart. Handsome. Magnificent. Muscular and altogether fantastic, yes, but not—"

Jessie grabbed his hair and dragged his mouth to hers. "I'll give you all the compliments you want, later. But first…" She sat up, tugged the sweatshirt over her head and tossed it aside. "Look at me, Liam," she said, "and tell me you like what you see."

Like? There were no words to describe what he felt, looking at her. Her body was as beautiful as her face, her skin all flushed, her breasts high and rounded, the tips already beaded with excitement.

"I love what I see," he said softly.

"Touch me, then." She reached up, stroked her finger gently over his mouth. "Kiss me. Make love to me."

He was on fire for her. Liam stripped off his jeans and shorts, and went into Jessie's arms. He'd dreamed of this, but the reality was better than any dream. The sweetness of her breasts, of her belly, the startled little sound she made when he opened her to him, found the secret flower that was the essence of her femininity and kissed it.

Her cry of shocked pleasure combined with her taste and rocketed through his blood. When she began to tremble, to convulse under the sweet torment of his mouth, he moved quickly up her body and, on one long, possessive stroke, sheathed himself in her satin heat.

"Jessie," he whispered, and when her lashes fluttered

open, he bent to her, cupped her face and kissed her deeply. "Look at me, sweetheart, and say my name."

"Liam. My Liam." A long, keening cry burst from her throat.

"Jessie," he said, and then he let go of everything, the years of loneliness and of doubt, and exploded deep within the welcoming warmth of the woman he loved.

CHAPTER SIX

JESSIE SAT on the sun-drenched patio, wearing a white, fluffy robe provided by the hotel and drinking coffee while she waited for Liam to return from what he'd smugly referred to as a "secret mission."

She smiled over the rim of her cup. It didn't take much effort to figure out what that "secret mission" was. She'd made a face when she'd started to dress, teased him about only men not shuddering at the thought of putting on yesterday's clothes, and he'd gotten a glint in his eyes. Suddenly he'd wanted to know her favorite colors, whether she liked short summer skirts or long ones, if she preferred bikinis or what he'd referred to as "you know, those clingy, one-piece jobs."

She put down her cup, stretched her arms high overhead, then lay back on the chaise longue.

He'd gone to buy her something to wear, she was sure of it. Still, she'd act surprised when he turned up with a swimsuit and a T-shirt and shorts and, yes, she'd stop being silly about it and accept them as gifts because it was pointless to stand on ceremony with the man who was your lover.

Her lover. She rolled over on her stomach and closed her eyes. It was such a lovely word. The only bit of darkness came when she let herself think about the emptiness she'd face when their days here ended.

And the pain she'd caused William.

"No," she said aloud.

She wasn't going to think about that, not yet. It was too soon to think about what lay ahead. She was happy, happier than she'd ever imagined possible, and she wasn't going to spoil her joy for anything.

She sat up, stretched again and took her coffee cup into the villa and rinsed it in the sink. The serving cart, bearing the remnants of the gargantuan breakfast Liam had ordered earlier, sat waiting in the corner. She thought of the waiter's smile when he'd delivered it, all that food for only two people, and how she'd felt herself blushing, knowing what he must have been thinking, that only a man and woman who'd spent hours making love could possibly be hungry enough to tackle waffles and eggs and a hundred other things.

And she thought of how Liam had taken her in his arms after the door closed, how they'd laughed while she fed him strips of bacon and he'd licked her fingers clean until laughter turned to sighs and sighs to passion.

She thought about how much she loved him.

There wasn't any point in trying to pretend she didn't, not to herself. It was impossible to fall in love with a man you hardly knew, especially when that man wasn't the kind she'd ever imagined wanting, but there it was. She loved Liam the way she'd wanted to love William, and what good would it do her?

"None," she said softly as she sank down on the edge of the bed.

Liam loved making love with her. He loved holding her, and he even seemed to love being with her. But he didn't love her. He'd never love just one woman. That was just the way they were, the Liam Malones of this world. Her mother had told her once, probably in a moment of desperation, that she'd made a terrible mistake thinking she didn't have to hear her man say those simple words, and thinking she could be happy with one who preferred wandering the world to making a real home.

Not that she'd have to be concerned about any of that with Liam. Even if a miracle occurred, which it wouldn't, but even if it did, and Liam looked at her and said those magical words, "Jessie, I love you…"

Even if that happened, he could never be hers because the shadow of William, and what they'd done, would always be there, chilling their happiness.

Tears rolled down her cheeks, and wasn't that ridiculous? Here she sat, weeping because there wouldn't be a forever-after when that was exactly what she'd walked away from, choosing, instead, a few short, sweet days in Liam's arms.

Jessie sat up straight, scrubbed her knuckles over her eyes. Liam would be back soon and she didn't want him to see that she'd been crying, didn't want to waste whatever little time they had left on tears or recriminations or—

A knock sounded at the front door. He must have locked himself out. She dabbed at her eyes again, ran her hands through her hair and went to open the door. But it wasn't Liam on the steps, it was a bellman with a load of gaily wrapped boxes in his arms. There were more boxes in the Jeep he'd parked alongside the villa.

"Packages for you, Miss Warren."

"There must be some mistake. I didn't order—"

"No, ma'am. Mr. Malone did."

"But…" She stepped back as the bellman started past her. It took two trips before he'd transferred everything from the Jeep. Jessie looked from the boxes to the bellman's smiling face. "I don't—I'm afraid I don't have anything to—"

The man's smile broadened. "Mr. Malone took care of that." He put his hand to his forehead, flipped her a brisk salute. "Enjoy the day, ma'am."

Jessie nodded. "You, too," she said, or thought she said, as the door swung shut. For a few minutes she just stared at the packages. Then, carefully, she unwrapped one, then another and another. Silk skirts, cotton tops, cashmere shawls and lace underwear spilled onto the bed.

"Liam," she said, laughing with delight, "oh, you crazy, wonderful man."

She took off her robe, let it slip to the floor, pulled on a cropped white top and a long, gauzy skirt and looked at herself in the mirror. Her eyes were bright with pleasure, her mouth was pink from Liam's kisses, her hair was a mass of curls and waves. She hardly recognized herself. What had become of Jessica Warren? Who was this woman in the mirror, wearing such beautiful things, her hair loose, her feet bare, all propriety and dignity forgotten?

Jessie's smile faded. And how could a heart soar, then break, all in the same moment?

"Liam," she whispered, "how can I let you go?"

Falling in love wasn't supposed to be like this. But, oh God, it was.

FALLING IN LOVE wasn't supposed to be like this.

Liam walked slowly along the shoreline, his hands tucked into the pockets of his jeans. He'd left Jessie on the patio, lying sleepily in the sun after they'd consumed a room service breakfast so huge even he'd laughed, and he'd been the one who ordered it. It was just that she'd smiled and said "you" each time he'd asked her what she wanted for breakfast and he'd felt honor-bound to take her up on the offer. When he finally reached for the phone, he hardly knew his own name so he'd ordered waffles and eggs, pancakes and bacon, biscuits and toast, strawberries, mangoes and coffee.

They'd eaten on the patio, and it was a good thing the villas were heavily screened by bougainvillea, because when Liam groaned and said he couldn't eat another mouthful, Jessie made a stern face and said he had to finish what he'd ordered. Laughing, she'd fed him a strip of crisp bacon. But when he reached the final bit and sucked her fingers into his mouth, her laughter had died, and they'd made love on the chaise longue, with the hot sun beating down.

Great. He was thinking what it was like to make love with Jessie and turning himself on.

"Malone," he said lightly, under his breath, "you're some piece of work."

Indeed, he was. He was a man in love, and the world had suddenly turned into a wonderful place, and never mind the gray smudge on the horizon, or the brisk breeze. It was a beautiful day, and it would be even more beautiful in—he looked at his watch—in just about five minutes, when the things he'd ordered were delivered to the villa.

After he and Jessie had finished breakfast and made love, they'd showered together. Liam gritted his teeth and told himself not to think about the way Jessie's skin felt wet, or how her hair streamed down over her breasts, or how he'd soaped her body, all of it, all of her....

He cleared his throat.

They'd put on the robes the hotel provided. Jessie had scooped up her clothing and wrinkled her nose.

"What?" Liam had asked, and she'd laughed and said that only a man would look so perplexed when a woman shuddered at the thought of taking a shower and then putting on the same stuff she'd worn the previous day. He'd clapped his hand to his heart, as if she'd wounded him deeply, accused her of being the female equivalent of a chauvinist pig, admitted she was probably right before dropping a kiss on her smiling lips. Then he'd put on his jeans and sweatshirt. "Stay just the way you are," he'd warned, "while I undertake a dark and dangerous secret mission."

And, he thought with smug assurance, he had.

He'd walked to the main building. First, he'd seen to his own things. He kept simple clothing—jeans, T-shirts, chinos and a blazer—in the owner's suite. He'd packed some of it and arranged for delivery to the villa. Then he'd gone to the gift shop and, well, maybe he'd gone just a little bit overboard.

"I need some things for a lady," he'd told the clerk. "She's…" He'd held his hand up, just about at mid-chest. "She's, uh, maybe so tall. And…" He'd started making curves in the air while the clerk watched politely and he felt his face turning red. "And she's, I don't know, a size six or maybe an eight. Her hips are…well, her waist is…"

The clerk had finally shown him some pity. "Lisa," she'd called, and a girl had come out of what he figured was the stockroom, a pretty girl about Jessie's height and weight. "Is the lady similar to Lisa, Mr. Malone?"

"Yes," Liam had answered, because he knew better than to think anybody wanted to hear him babble that Jessie wasn't similar to any other woman in the world.

The clerk had dismissed Lisa with an imperious wave of the hand. "What kinds of 'things' did you have in mind, sir?"

Shorts, he'd told her, and T-shirts. Oh, and a swimsuit. And how about a couple of those long filmy skirts? Those little cotton tops? Those silk things, with the lace?

"Camisoles," the clerk had said with a quick smile.

"Camisoles, right. And sandals. And that dress, the one with the little flowers." He'd paused at a counter, picked up a little vial, opened it, sniffed it, smelled lilacs. "This, too," he'd said, "and that. And this—"

In the end, he'd ordered too much to carry, so he'd arranged for it to be delivered.

"Your lady is a lucky woman," the clerk had said, and Liam had replied that he was the lucky one....

It wasn't true.

His smile fled. He bent down, plucked a small white stone from the sand and threw it far out into the surf. He wasn't lucky, because this couldn't last. Jessie had made love with him, but she still belonged to another man. Not just any other man, either. She belonged to William.

Liam stared blindly over the water. Hell, no. Falling in love was not supposed to be like this.

He sighed and began walking again. Not that he was any kind of expert. Until now he'd figured love was a concept dreamed up by salesmen trying to sell soap. One man, one woman, bells ringing, fireworks going off— how could any of that be real?

But it was. You saw a woman, a special woman, and all that stuff happened. And if you were lucky, it was that way for her, too, so that both of you knew it could be like this for the rest of your lives. He knew, anyway, and even if Jessie hadn't said so, she knew it, too. It was there, in her eyes, in the way she kissed him, in everything she said and did.

She loved him, he loved her, and what could possibly come of it? Nothing but grief, all around.

"Dammit," Liam said. What else was there to say without putting back his head and howling his anguish to the gods who had to be looking down and laughing until their sides split? Fate sure had a hell of a sense of humor.

Liam Malone, who'd figured love was about parts of the body that hadn't a damn thing to do with the heart, who'd thought that even talking about settling down marked a man as a sucker extraordinaire—that very same Liam Malone was in love.

"Find my Jessica," Bill had said, "and do the right thing."

Liam mouthed an oath, kicked at the sand and watched the shiny particles rise into the air. Maybe the day wasn't as beautiful as he'd thought. Little whitecaps danced on the restless sea and that dark smudge in the distance was growing. The woman at the gift shop had mentioned that a storm might be blowing in.

"It won't last," she'd promised. "Trouble in paradise never does."

She had it wrong. What never lasted was paradise. How come he hadn't remembered that? Life had a way of holding out happiness, waiting until you reached for it and then snatching it back. He should have told that to the clerk—although it was probably just as well he hadn't. She'd only have looked at him as if he was nuts. Not a good thing, he thought with a little smile, for the staff to label the owner. Not that it seemed so great that he owned Flamingo Island or that he'd turned his life around.

It would only mean something if he could share it with Jessie.

He'd kept it a secret from Bill because he'd wanted to tell him in person, how he'd awakened one morning with a fortune in his wallet and a French movie star in his bed. He'd been on a hot streak that month, winning hand after hand at high-stakes poker tables, dazzling the oil barons and investment bankers he'd outplayed, and he'd opened his eyes that particular day, looked at the famous face on the pillow beside his, then at the opulent gold-leaf ceiling in his posh hotel suite, and said, "Malone, just what the hell are you doing?"

So he'd kissed the movie star goodbye, dumped his money into the startup stock of an Internet company he'd heard about over a hand of poker. Two weeks later, he cashed out, rich. Rich beyond his wildest dreams. But it became boring, reading the financial news and watching his money make more money. He took a chunk of it, looked around for opportunities, bought this place for no better reason than that he found it peaceful and beautiful. The next thing he knew, he'd turned himself into a man he'd thought he'd never want to be. To his amazement, he liked the transformation—but he'd never planned on falling in love. Love hadn't worked for his parents, who'd probably died screaming at each other as their car hit the overpass abutment, or for the rich and famous he'd known over the last decade.

Except it had happened. With Jessie, the only woman he'd ever love. He'd tell her that, slowly. Work up to it, because as much as he loved her, it scared him.

The villa door swung open. Jessie smiled at him. She had on one of the outfits he'd bought, a little white top with a long, filmy skirt, and she'd left her hair loose, the way he liked it.

"Jessie," he blurted. "Sweetheart, I'm crazy in love with you."

She didn't say anything. Then, just when he thought he'd made the worst mistake a man could ever make, she threw herself into his arms.

"Liam," she said. "Oh, Liam, I was so afraid it was only me."

He swept her up, kicked the door shut and, for a little while, nothing mattered but showing each other exactly what being in love meant.

THEY LAY IN EACH OTHER'S ARMS in the center of the bed, safe and secure in the aftermath of their lovemaking.

Liam inhaled the fragrance of Jessie's hair. "You smell delicious. Is that the perfume I gave you?"

"Mmm-hmm. It's lovely."

"And what you were wearing. I loved you in that. You know, the long skirt and that top, the one that looks like somebody shrank it."

She laughed softly and snuggled closer. "You must have emptied out that gift shop."

Liam took her hand from his chest and brought it to his lips. "Did I buy the right size? If there's anything you don't like—"

"Everything was perfect, but I can't let you spend so much money on me."

"I'd give you the world, if you'd let me."

Jessie lifted her head from his shoulder and kissed his mouth. "Thank you," she said softly. "But even if the cards have been good to you lately—"

"Aha." Liam grinned. "So, Bill told, and the deep, dark secret's out, huh? That I used to be a gambler?"

"Uh-huh. Give you a deck of cards and you're…used to be?"

"That's right, sweetheart." He rolled over, gently eased her onto her back. "I've reformed."

"A reformed rogue." Jessie touched the tip of her finger to his mouth. "William will be pleased to…I mean, that's nice to hear." She smiled, though the smile was wobbly. "But I can't see you working nine to five."

"People change." A muscle knotted in his jaw. "You think you know exactly who you are and what you want out of life. Then, I don't know, you walk down a street or read a book…" He cleared his throat. "Or you agree to be the best man at an old friend's wedding, and—"

"Don't." Jessie put her hand over Liam's mouth. "Please," she whispered, "not yet."

"We have to talk about it. You know that."

"Yes. But—"

"I love you with all my heart, Jess." His voice was deep, his words a whisper. "I want you to know I've never said those words to another woman, and I never will."

"Liam. Oh, God, Liam—" Her voice broke. "What are we going to do? I thought—I thought this was just a—a…. I don't know what I thought. When I first saw you—"

"I know. It was the same for me."

"It terrified me but I told myself it was only—that it was only—"

"Sex," Liam said softly. "Yeah, so did I. A couple of hours in bed." He pulled Jessie into his arms and held her close. "Then I got on that plane and saw the way you looked at me. Or maybe it was when I undressed you and you went into my arms so trustingly. I only know that I love you, that I'll always love—"

Jessie pressed her mouth to his. He could taste her tears in her kiss.

"I'll always love you, too," she whispered. "But—but you know that this is all we can ever have."

"No! Don't say that." He sat up. "I want to marry you, Jessie. I want to do all those things I never believed in. Buy a house. Have kids. Live happily ever after. Sweetheart, don't you understand? Without you—"

"My life will be empty, too." The words shuddered from her lips. "I tried to tell myself we could make a life together, Liam. But we can't. William will always be between us." She began to weep. "You know what we have to do."

He did know. Each beat of his heart reminded him of his promise to Bill. "I'll do the right thing," he'd said. But the right thing had changed. The world had changed. Right was wrong, and promises were pain.

"I'm not giving you up," Liam said fiercely.

"You love William as much as I do, and he adores you." She took an unsteady breath. "You're his hero."

"God." He let go of her, sat up and raked his fingers through his hair. "Some hero I turned out to be."

"He told me once that you and I are the two most important people in his life." Jessie knelt beside Liam and took his hand. "It would be bad enough if one of us let him down, but if—if we betray him—"

Liam couldn't listen to any more. She was right but he wouldn't admit it, not to her, not to himself. Instead, he sprang to his feet.

"There's got to be a way!" He grabbed his jeans and stepped into them. "My mind's going in circles. I have to take a walk." He stopped and took Jessie's hands. "I'll come up with something. I'm not going to lose you, Jess. Not after I spent my life looking for you."

Jessie laughed, but by the time she rose from the bed and put her arms around him, her laughter had turned to tears.

"I know," she sobbed. "I'll never forget you, or this time we spent together. I'll always adore you, Liam, always."

He kissed her as if the world were going to end at any moment. And, in a way, it did, because when he returned to the villa less than an hour later, Jessie was gone.

CHAPTER SEVEN

RAIN BEAT DOWN on the island, and a driving wind rattled the fronds of the palm trees that towered over the villa.

Inside, a grim-faced Liam faced three hapless hotel employees.

"It's a simple question," he said coldly. "Surely one of you can answer it."

The desk clerk who'd arranged for Jessie's flight to Miami, the driver who'd taken her to the airstrip, even the chambermaid who'd gone to the villa hours ago to make the bed and had ended up, instead, directing Jessie to the office, looked at him, then at each other. No one spoke. Finally the desk clerk shifted his feet.

"I've explained, sir. The young lady phoned the desk. She said she wanted to leave the island. She asked—"

"I know what she asked," Liam snapped. "What I'm having difficulty with is that you didn't think to inform me."

"I'm sorry, sir. There didn't seem to be any..." The clerk licked his lips. "We—we didn't know that you'd object." He looked to his companions for support. Both of them were nodding their heads vigorously. "We were only doing what your guest asked us to do, sir."

"I see." Liam folded his arms and glared at the man. "Do you always do what guests ask you to do?"

The clerk swallowed dryly. "We—we try to accommodate all requests, Mr. Malone."

"Suppose a guest wanted to jump off the roof? Would you let her do that?"

"No, sir. Certainly not. But—"

You're acting like an idiot, Liam said to himself, while the clerk stumbled for words. Just what was it he expected these people to have done? Tell Jessie she couldn't fly out without permission? Wait for him to give his okay? Guests of the hotel were supposed to be treated with courtesy, and they'd done that. As for Jessie—she'd done what had to be done, what he hadn't had the courage to do despite his promise to Bill, and now he was venting his anger on these poor people rather than dealing with the truth.

He and Jessie could never have a life together. One of them, at least, understood the meaning of the word *honor.*

"—did the best we could, sir, by accommodating the lady's wishes, and—"

"That's okay," Liam said, interrupting the clerk's stumbling explanation. "You're right. I'm wrong." He dredged up a smile. "In fact, I was way out of line."

Color began seeping back into the man's face. "If we'd known you wanted us to speak with you first, Mr. Malone—"

"Forget it. It's a free country. The lady wanted to leave and that's that." Liam clasped the man's shoulder, then shook hands with all three employees. "There'll be something extra in your paychecks this week," he said briskly, and herded them to the door. "How's that sound?"

"Thank you," they said, "thank you very much, Mr.—"

Liam shut the door, let the smile slip from his mouth and sank down on the edge of the bed. After a moment, he buried his face in his hands. Jessie was gone and he couldn't go after her even if he wanted to. The smudge on the horizon had turned into a charcoal bank of clouds, spewing rain and wind. Until the weather cleared, there was no way off the island.

Besides, what was the sense in going after her? Their affair had been doomed from the beginning. Jessie had said it all in the last few minutes they'd been together.

"You're his hero, Liam."

Liam groaned and fell back against the pillows. Oh, yeah. He was Bill's hero, all right.

If only he'd met Jessie a year ago. Six months ago. Hell, a day before Bill put that ring on her finger would have been enough. What a difference that little bit of time would have made. He and Jessie would have met, there'd have been that same wild, lightning-hot attraction....

No. He wasn't going to do that, play a game of "if only" that would do nothing but make the pain worse. Liam sat up and scrubbed his hands over his face. He'd lost Jessie, lost her forever....

To hell with that. Bill was his oldest friend, yes, but Jessie—Jessie was everything.

He sprang from the bed, grabbed his leather jacket,

reached for the phone. No way was he going to lose her. He loved her. He adored her. He…

He had no right to her.

The jacket fell from his hand. There was no way around the truth. He'd betrayed Bill, made a promise he hadn't kept. Now he had to go back, face Bill as Jessie was going to do, admit his guilt and ask his forgiveness before fading out of the picture. Anything else—like loving Jessie— he'd relegate to the past.

Liam lifted his head. He could hear the faint sound of an airplane engine in the distance. He went to the door, opened it, looked up into a clear, rain-washed night sky. The small plane that ferried guests to and from the island, that had taken Jessie from him, forever, was coming in for a landing. He could tell the pilot to gas it up, turn it around.

Not yet.

Tomorrow was soon enough to fly west. Once he did, it would all be over. Could it really be only a couple of days since he'd first seen Jessie, days that had changed his life, forever?

Liam sank down on the bed again, lay back and put his arm over his eyes. *Jessie,* he thought, *Jessie, my love.*

Early the next morning, he was on a flight headed for Seattle.

IN MOST PARTS OF THE COUNTRY spring meant flowers, sunshine and birdsong. In Seattle, tucked between the rainforests of the Olympic Peninsula and the towering Cascade Mountains, spring meant rain.

Jessie had never minded that. She'd heard some people

say the gray skies were depressing, but she loved the misty feel of the air, and those moments when the clouds parted and Mount Rainier was visible on the horizon always made her spirits lift.

Nothing could make that happen, not this spring.

Except for a stop at her bank, where she'd picked up a new ATM card and used it to take some money from her account, and then an hour spent buying a few things to wear, she'd been huddled in her hotel room ever since she'd arrived in the city. She'd intended to face William immediately but once she stepped into the hotel, she'd realized she had to get herself in hand first. She felt as if her life had stopped when the plane carrying her away from Liam lifted into the air. She'd watched their villa recede and then the hotel until, finally, the island had been only a small dot in the vast ocean.

"Liam," she'd whispered, and she'd wept for what could never be, the lifetime of love they might have shared. If only they'd met some other time, some other place.

Jessie sighed.

Perhaps not.

What she'd shared with Liam couldn't possibly last. She'd always known that. Such fire, such heat, would only burn out over time. For all she knew, it had already turned to cold ashes, otherwise why wouldn't Liam have come after her?

No. No, she didn't want him to do that. She wanted to set things right. If William was willing to take her back, she'd—she'd…

She'd never let it happen.

Yes, she'd beg his forgiveness, tell him he was a wonderful man and that he deserved to find a woman who'd make him happy, but she wasn't that woman. She loved Liam. She always would, for the rest of her life, even though she'd never see him again.

A sob caught in her throat.

"God," Jessie whispered, "help me, please."

She reached for the phone, punched in the number for the big house on the lake before she had too much time to think about what she was doing. Her heart was thumping; her hand was so wet her fingers slipped on the plastic handpiece. Who would answer? The maid? The cook? Or William, himself. What would she say to him? What—

"Thornton residence."

Jessie blinked. "Carrie?"

"Jessica?"

"Yes. It's…did I dial the wrong number? I'm sorry. I've been so—so upset that—"

"*You've* been upset?" Carrie gave a cold laugh. "I hardly think so. William's the one who's upset."

Jessie closed her eyes. "I know."

"You don't know. How could you, when you and that man have been—have been…"

"William—William knows about—about Liam?"

"Certainly he knows. That man called from the airport. We know you and he flew to Florida. Together."

Each word was a brand and an accusation. "Carrie." Jessie took a breath, expelled it and rose to her feet. "Put William on the phone, please."

"I don't know that he'll want to talk with you."

"Maybe not. But ask him, will you?"

"He's busy. If he has time later, maybe he'll call you back."

The line went dead. Slowly, Jessie hung up the phone. William couldn't call, not without her phone number, and Carrie hadn't requested it.

Something had changed while she'd been gone, some delicate shift of power and loyalty. Jessie thought about it for a minute. Not that it mattered. William might, in fact, despise her, refuse to see her. He certainly had the right.

Still, she had to face him.

Jessie put on her jacket, picked up her car keys and locked the door to her room behind her.

LIAM PULLED TO THE CURB just before Bill's driveway and sat staring straight ahead as the car idled.

"Come on, Malone," he muttered, "get it together."

He had to before he faced Bill. It had all seemed so clear back on Flamingo Island. Confront Bill, explain that what had happened was nobody's fault but his, that he'd never intended to betray their friendship, wish him well and walk away. He'd worked it all out during a couple of endless hours spent pacing the first-class lounge at the Miami airport, refined it during almost six hours of flying time.

So how come he still didn't know what he'd say when Bill opened the door?

Liam smiled grimly. All things considered, he might not have to worry about it. He'd ring the bell, Bill would open the door and their conversation would begin and end with Bill delivering a hard right to Liam's jaw.

That was what he'd do, if a man stole Jessie from him. Not that one punch would do it. He'd want to kill the bastard. Jessie was his. She'd always be his. Nobody could ever take her from…

Liam crossed his hands on the steering wheel and pressed his forehead to his wrists.

She wasn't his. That was the point of this whole infuriating exercise. He'd come back to acknowledge the truth, that he had no claim on Jessie, even though he'd never stop loving her, that he was the worst friend a man had ever had, a lying, cheating, double-dealing, no-good bastard.

"Just admit you're a rat," he muttered, "and then get the hell out."

He straightened in his seat, put the car in gear, shot up the driveway—and looked up just in time to see a small white car come hurtling up behind him.

"Son of a—"

He jammed his foot on the brake pedal, felt the jolt and heard the glass breaking as the white car's headlights shattered. He threw open the door and jumped out.

"Damned idiot," he snarled, as he strode toward the other car. "Where'd you learn to drive?" This jerk needed driving lessons. That was fine. Better than fine, considering his mood. If Bill slugged him, he couldn't slug back, but if this idiot so much as made a sound—

"Get out of there," Liam said. He yanked open the door, reached in…and saw Jessie. Her face was pale, her eyes were red rimmed. From tears, he knew, because he'd cried, too, in his heart, and he knew, too, that the person he'd really been lying to was himself.

No matter what happened, he would never let her leave him again.

"Jessie," he said, and she was in his arms before her name had left his lips.

"Liam," she sobbed. "Oh, Liam, my love."

"Why did you leave me?"

"Why didn't you come after me?"

"I didn't want to leave you, but—"

"I wanted to go after you, but—"

They spoke together, words, voices, crossing in a hurried blur. Then they fell silent. Liam's arms tightened around her, Jessie raised her face and they kissed.

"I love you," Liam said fiercely against her mouth. "And I'm not letting you go."

"Don't." She sighed. "Oh, don't. Not ever. I need you, Liam, I need you and love you and—"

The door to the house swung open. Liam and Jessie turned and saw Bill and Carrie standing in the entrance. Jessie started to pull away, but Liam kept an arm around her waist, anchoring her to him.

"Well," Carrie said, "isn't this a pretty sight?"

Liam ignored her. "Bill," he said steadily.

Bill Thornton's expression was unreadable. "Liam."

"William," Jessie said, "William, I'm so sorry."

"It's my fault," Liam said. "Not hers." He dropped his arm from Jessie's waist and took her hand. Her fingers were icy, and he squeezed them reassuringly. "Jessie had nothing to do with what happened."

Bill's mouth thinned. "How noble."

"Bill, look. Neither of us planned this. I mean, we didn't expect…"

"And that's supposed to make it okay?" He took a step forward. "My best friend. And my fiancée. What a fine pair you make."

"William." Jessie's voice broke. "We never meant to hurt you. You have to believe that."

"The only thing I have to believe is that I never knew either one of you. I'd have trusted you with my life, Liam. And Jessica…I thought you were the most wonderful woman in the world, but now—"

"Watch what you say to her," Liam said, his voice hardening. "I'm the one who made a mess of things, understand? You want to take a shot at me, go ahead."

Bill stared at the two of them, then shrugged his shoulders. "What would be the point? It wouldn't change anything." A tired smile lifted one corner of his mouth. "Besides, the last time I tried that, Malone, I ended up almost needing to have my jaw wired shut, remember?"

Some of the tension eased from Liam's stance. "Yeah, but that was ten years ago, and you were dumb enough to think you could tackle me five yards from the goalpost."

"It was just a game of pickup football," Bill said. His eyes went to Jessie, then back to Liam. "You weren't defending something as basic as your right to fall in love with Jessica." He cleared his throat. "That's what this is all about, isn't it? You're in love with her."

Liam's jaw knotted. "Yes."

"And you, Jessica? Do you love him, too?"

"Yes," Jessie whispered. "I love him with all my heart." Tears rose in her eyes. "But you'll always be special to me, William. I want you to know that."

"Special," Bill said, and gave a bitter laugh. "And I'm supposed to take comfort in that?"

"I promised you I'd do the right thing," Liam said, his eyes steady on Bill's. "It's true, I made some detours along the way, but in the end, I know that what I'm doing now *is* the right thing." He paused, twined his fingers through Jessie's. "I love Jessie. And she loves me. She can't marry you because it would be a travesty. Everyone would end up cheated—you, me, and her—and not one of us would be able to live down the shame for the rest of our lives."

After a long moment, Bill sighed. "I guess that's one of life's toughest lessons, that the right thing isn't always easy to figure out."

"No," Liam agreed, "it isn't."

"Anyway, I'm not blameless. Part of this mess is my fault, too."

"That's not true," Carrie said, with indignation. "You didn't do anything!"

"But I did." Bill took Carrie's hand and held it tightly. "I didn't give Jessica any options. One night she agreed to have dinner with me and the next thing she knew, I was making her part of my life. Isn't that right, Jessica?"

"If you mean that you were wonderful…" Jessie smiled shakily. "You sent me flowers every day. You phoned all the time."

"Sure. I figured if you were right for me, all I had to

do was convince you that I was right for you. I guess I thought, well, if we were a great team in the office, we'd be terrific as husband and wife." He cleared his throat. "Obviously, I was wrong."

"Bill." Liam cleared his throat, too. "I don't expect you to forgive us—"

"Good." Bill stood straight and tall, and looked directly into Liam's eyes. "Because I haven't. You want the truth, Malone? I don't know if I'll ever forgive you. Accepting what's happened is one thing. Forgiving it is another."

Liam nodded. "I understand. Let's—let's give it some time, okay?"

"Yeah," Bill said, "let's do that."

He stepped back, still clasping Carrie's hand, and the door swung shut. Liam stood motionless for a long moment. Then he swallowed hard, turned to Jessie and took her in his arms. She was weeping, and he drew her close and kissed away her tears.

"Don't cry," he said softly. "It's going to be okay."

"Poor William. He's so hurt." She sniffled, and Liam dug out his handkerchief and handed it to her. "He was right, you know." She smiled through her tears. "We were a great team in the office. We should have left it at that."

Liam smiled, too, as he took her in his arms again. "You liked being assistant to the CEO, huh?"

"Yes." Despite her tears, she tilted her chin in defiance. "Don't tell me you're one of those male chauvinists, Malone, who doesn't like the idea of his woman having a job."

"To begin with," Liam said gently, "you're not going to be my woman, you're going to be my wife."

Jessie sighed. "I like the sound of that."

"And you're right, I don't like the idea of you working for some guy."

"Now, wait a minute, Liam—"

Liam kissed her. "Working *with* some guy," he said, smiling into her eyes, "an equal partnership kind of thing, well, that's different."

"What are you talking about? Do you mean you're thinking of starting some sort of business?" She snuggled against him. "Oh, that would be lovely. But you don't have to do it for me. I know you like to bounce from place to place, and if that's what you want, it's what we'll do."

Liam wrapped his hand around the back of her neck and tilted her face to his. "I have a lot to tell you, sweetheart. About me, about my life…" He could feel his heart lift. "Let's just say I've got some irons in the fire that can use your skills and, no, we're not going to bounce from place to place, unless that's what you really want."

"I just want you," Jessie whispered. "Only you, my love."

"Always," Liam said softly. "For all the rest of our lives."

EPILOGUE

THEY WERE MARRIED less than a month later, in the solarium of the handsome house they'd bought on one of the beautiful San Juan Islands in Puget Sound.

Jessie had wanted to be wed in the garden, because a garden was where they'd met, but Liam convinced her to take pity on their guests and have the ceremony inside the solarium. The northwest was still in the grip of a chilly spring, but that day the sun shone. The first of the spring crocuses had pushed their heads through the snow and Jessie had decorated both the house and the solarium in the same soft lilac color.

She wore white silk; Liam wore a black tux. A guitarist played softly in the background. There was champagne and caviar, oysters and Dungeness crab, and on top of the five-tiered wedding cake, in place of the figures of a bride and groom, there stood a small globe that Liam had given Jessie at breakfast.

It was made of crystal and, inside it, a tiny porcelain bride who looked suspiciously like her, and a porcelain groom who more than resembled Liam, embraced before a bright green palm tree standing on white sand, set against a tropical cardboard sea.

Jessie had wept with happiness.

"Turn it over," Liam had said gently. She did, and as the sand turned the placid scene into a hurricane, she saw the inscription engraved on the bottom of the globe.

Let The World Tilt, it said.

Now, the ceremony that would join them forever was moments away. Their future stretched ahead, brightly shining. There had been some difficult moments as Jessie's friends made peace with the fact that she'd fallen in love with another man on what was to have been her wedding day, but she and Liam were so much in love that no one could fault her, or him, for following the dictates of their hearts. And they were filled with plans, plans that Liam had already put into motion. He was CEO of Flamingo Resorts; she was Chief Financial Officer. They worked together, played together, loved together.

Their lives had taken the shape fate had meant them to take all along.

And it would all be perfect, Jessie thought, as she stood in the encircling curve of her husband's arm—they'd both agreed that they didn't want to be separated, not even for the hours prior to their wedding. It would be perfect, but for one thing.

"You're thinking about Bill," she said softly.

Liam nodded. It was the first time she'd referred to William by his nickname. Liam knew that, in some subtle way, it marked a passage in their lives.

"Yeah," he said. "I am. I didn't really expect him to come." He ran an index finger under his collar. "I just thought—"

"Liam?"

"I thought, well, maybe he'd realize that our friend-ship—"

"Liam." Jessie looked up at Liam and smiled. "He's here, darling."

Liam stiffened, then looked across the room. Bill and Carrie were coming toward them. A huge smile broke over his face.

"Bill." He stepped forward. "Man, I'm so happy you—"

"Me, too."

The men stared at each other. Then Liam held out his hand and Bill clasped it.

"Good to see you," Bill said.

"Yeah." Liam grinned. "Same here."

Bill let go of Liam's hand and drew a smiling Carrie forward. "We're engaged, Carrie and I." He looped his arm around her shoulders. "Crazy, isn't it? That so much good came out of this whole thing?"

"I think it's wonderful." Jessie touched her cheek to Carrie's. Then she took Liam's arm and smiled at the others. "Just wonderful."

"So," Bill said briskly, after a moment had gone by, "what's the deal here, huh? Did you manage to bribe some poor slob into standing up for you?"

Liam laughed, though Jessie noticed his green eyes were suspiciously bright.

"Actually, I figured, why go to all that trouble when the best man of my choice was going to show up any minute?"

Bill grinned. "You really sure you want to do this, Malone? Sign your freedom away to one woman?"

"Absolutely." Liam turned to Jessie and took her in his arms. "For all of my life."

Jessie smiled. "Forever," she said, and kissed the only man she had ever, would ever, love.

There are 24 timeless classics in the Mills & Boon® 100th Birthday Collection

Two of these beautiful stories are out each month. Make sure you collect them all!

If you have missed any of these books, log on to www.millsandboon.co.uk to order your copies online.